"Good
morning,
Amane-
san."

KISARAGI CLAIRE

NINETEEN YEARS OLD. A MEMBER OF THE
YOIZUKI GUILD AND AN S-RANK ADVENTURER
WHO'S RANKED TWELFTH IN JAPAN. SHE USES A
WEAPON CALLED THE ICE BURIAL SWORD.

THE WORLD'S FASTEST
LEVEL UP

"Absolute Ruler."

She summoned an ice magic circle around
herself, large enough to surround me,
Hana, and everyone else as well.
Massive amounts of mana spilled from it.

"No way..." I muttered, eyes wide.
Our near-fatal wounds had healed in
the blink of an eye.

"Piece Ruler."

The very fabric and workings of the world as we know it will be overwritten.

"I'll level up right here, right now, and try to obtain a new skill!"

CAIN FON VERTIA

THE BLOODSUCKING KING, A MAN WHO BENDS THE VITAL FLUID OF LIFE—THAT IS, RUBY-RED BLOOD—TO HIS WHIMS. IN THE DEEPEST DEPTHS OF A NEW DUNGEON, HE LIES IN WAIT FOR RIN AND HIS FRIENDS.

AMANE RIN

AWAKENED TO THE UNIQUE SKILL "DUNGEON TELEPORTATION," HE IS THE ONLY ADVENTURER IN THE WORLD TO WHOM THE RULES DO NOT APPLY.

THE WORLD'S FASTEST
LEVEL ⌃ UP

SEKAI SAISOKU NO LEVEL UP Vol. 3
©Nagato Yamata, fame 2022
First published in Japan in 2022 by
KADOKAWA CORPORATION, Tokyo.
English translation rights arranged with
KADOKAWA CORPORATION, Tokyo.

Seven Seas press and purchase enquiries can be sent to
Marketing Manager Lianne Sentar at press@gomanga.com.
Information regarding the distribution and purchase of
digital editions is available from Digital Manager CK Russell
at digital@gomanga.com.

Follow Seven Seas Entertainment online at
sevenseasentertainment.com.

TRANSLATION: Morgan Watchorn
ADAPTATION: Nikita Greene
COVER DESIGN: Nicky Lim
LOGO DESIGN: George Panella
INTERIOR LAYOUT & DESIGN: Clay Gardner
COPY EDITOR: Meg van Huygen
PROOFREADER: Dayna Abel
LIGHT NOVEL EDITOR: Mercedez Clewis
PREPRESS TECHNICIAN: Melanie Ujimori, Jules Valera
PRODUCTION MANAGER: Lissa Pattillo
EDITOR-IN-CHIEF: Julie Davis
ASSOCIATE PUBLISHER: Adam Arnold
PUBLISHER: Jason DeAngelis

ISBN: 978-1-68579-644-0
Printed in Canada
First Printing: May 2023
10 9 8 7 6 5 4 3 2 1

THE WORLD'S FASTEST
LEVEL UP

NOVEL
3

WRITTEN BY
NAGATO
YAMATA

ILLUSTRATED BY
fame

Airship

Seven Seas Entertainment

THE WORLD'S FASTEST LEVEL UP

CONTENTS

009	PROLOGUE	
015	CHAPTER 1	YOIZUKI AND THE STRONGEST
041	CHAPTER 2	EXPLOSIVE SPEED LEVELING
091	CHAPTER 3	TEAM DIVE
119	CHAPTER 4	DEVOURING THE STRONG
131	CHAPTER 5	A REASON TO FIGHT
153	CHAPTER 6	TURNING POINT
179	CHAPTER 7	SILVER AND BLUE
203	CHAPTER 8	THE TYRANT AND THE KING
221	CHAPTER 9	A SMALL GLORY
231	EPILOGUE	
239	AFTERWORD	

PROLOGUE

A FEW HOURS BEFORE *I met Claire...*

Hana was off to school, and I was prepping my gear before I headed out. Today, I planned to return to the Remote Magic Tower and test whether I could reenter it using Dungeon Teleportation. If I succeeded, a few days of fierce battle were ahead of me. That required my usual careful preparation.

While I worked, the TV replayed a major news story.

"Just days ago, an adventurer shocked the world by becoming the youngest person to surpass level 100,000. She's now rewritten history by achieving S-rank..."

I couldn't get away from this omnipresent news story; I was seriously sick of it. With a click, I turned the TV off and sped up my preparations. I didn't have time to worry about what other people were attaining if I wanted to be stronger than them *and* do it faster.

"Okay, ready to go!" I said and set out for the Remote Magic Tower.

Yet, for some reason, that news story replayed over and over in my mind. I couldn't say why—until, as if it was a premonition, I met that very special S-rank adventurer a few hours later.

◆ ⌃ ◆

A little further back, the day before Claire met Amane Rin...

Claire, a stunning girl with long silver hair and intense blue eyes, entered the Yoizuki guild master's office.

"Master, you summoned me?" she asked.

"Yes. Thanks for coming, Claire."

The man in the chair paused his busy hands and looked up, abandoning the stack of documents on his desk. Among the documents was a single photograph of a person, which caught Claire's eye. The guild master made an inquisitive sound as he followed her gaze and realized what it fell on.

"Are you curious about him?" he asked.

"Not him specifically. I'm just wondering why there's a picture among those documents."

"If you're that curious, take it, please! Call it a present of sorts."

"...You're not listening."

Exasperated as she was, Claire took the picture. It showed a boy with short black hair and dark, focused eyes. She scrutinized the photo, but she couldn't place him.

"Who is he?" she asked.

"Ah, Amane Rin."

"Amane Rin... That name came up when I inquired about the Kenzaki dungeon collapse the other day. Why would you give his picture to me?"

"Good question. I want to try recruiting him to join the guild again and I want *you* to do it directly."

She inclined her head. "Recruit him? I thought you said he wasn't very strong."

"On the surface, he wasn't."

"Only on the surface?"

"I think Amane Rin's hiding what he can really do."

"And your basis for that assumption is *what*, exactly?" Claire asked gravely.

He showed her a document. The title read: "Murder Occurs During Dungeon Practice Session."

"This refers to the murder of that Association staff member, right? You think Amane Rin is connected to it somehow?"

"That's the big question. He's entangled in it to some degree but... what I'm about to say must stay completely between us," he warned.

He explained the circumstances of the incident: Monsters had spawned during the practice session, then a staff member named Yanagi stayed to stop them and allow the students to escape. Unfortunately, Amane Rin's little sister, Hana, was left behind. A different staff member named Katagiri went back for her, but only Hana emerged alive. In the aftermath, Yanagi and Katagiri's bodies were found by Dungeon Association staff. As for where Amane Rin came in, he hadn't participated in the practice, but he *was* at the scene after the incident.

The guild master's summary made Claire doubtful of his theory.

"I see. So his sister was directly involved," she mused. "But if there's nothing else abnormal about the situation, then perhaps he could've simply been contacted about her and rushed to the scene?"

"You're not necessarily wrong. It could be coincidence, but there's *another* mystery at play."

He slid a second photograph toward her. This one showed a magic stone slab.

"There's something special about this...?" Claire examined the photo closely. "Are those *letters* engraved into it?"

"That's right. This magic slab was left beside the bodies of the deceased staff members and monsters. It details what transpired and implicates Yanagi as the killer. It claims he possessed a unique skill called Plunderer that allowed him to kill people and steal their skills. Katagiri was a victim of Yanagi, so someone had to have killed him and left the slab behind."

"Hmm. They went out of their way to leave it?"

The guild master nodded. "Baffling, isn't it? It's possible that both staff members are victims and the culprit left it behind to toy with the investigation. Though, if you think about it, leaving *nothing* behind would have left much less evidence for the investigators to work with. That leads me to believe the story engraved here is real, and the person who killed Yanagi couldn't let him get away with his crimes."

The guild master lifted another document and continued.

"Multiple people with unique skills have died under strange circumstances lately—and Yanagi was proven to be connected with all of them in some way. The Association also seems to believe the story is true."

Claire rubbed her chin in thought. "Noted. If that's the case, this mystery person slipped out of the dungeon *after* the fatal fight. It makes sense they would've emerged before the Dungeon Association investigated..."

"And Amane Rin appeared *before* the investigation. I don't know how he got in and out of the dungeon, but it wouldn't be impossible if he had the right skill. He had plenty of reason to do so, especially to save his sister. Well? Not such a bad theory, is it?"

Claire still wasn't satisfied. "It's a solid theory, but let's say it's correct and Amane Rin-san actually *does* have promising power. I heard Yanagi and those monsters were each over level 10,000. Was he capable of defeating them by himself?"

The question was so obvious, it almost went without saying. According to the guild master, Amane Rin only had one year of adventuring under his belt. No rational adventurer would casually suggest that much power was obtainable in so little time.

The guild master nodded confidently, throwing rationality out the window. "I *do* think he's capable. His unique skill is a type of teleportation we haven't seen before."

Claire's eyes widened. "Teleportation? That's an incredible power."

"Isn't it?" His excitement was rising. "When he was just a fledgling adventurer, it was useless, but who knows how it evolved as he leveled up. I think there's a high chance that he's the one who defeated the Kenzaki boss too! Can you guess why?"

"Because, if he teleported, he could've entered the sealed boss room?"

"*Bingo.*" He grinned.

She couldn't just leave it at that. "If you're correct, I understand why he would hide his abilities. I, too, personally understand the devastation too much power can cause. But why am I the best one to recruit him?"

"Well...I figure a cute girl like yourself would be more convincing than an old man like me, and as my daughter, you're the absolute cutest girl in the whole world!"

"I see you have no intention of answering my question seriously. That said, since I'm somewhat curious about him, I'll accept."

"Oho? How rare for you to take an interest in other people! Regardless, that'll be a big help. This is the Amane family's address. The rest is in your hands."

She accepted the paper with Amane Rin's address, unsure where the guild master had learned it. Granted, Yoizuki *was* the most famous guild in the area—it had deep ties with the Dungeon Association and the government, so a paltry task like finding an address could get done before breakfast.

Address and photograph in hand, Claire left the building and marched straight for Amane Rin's home.

"Amane Rin-san..." she mused. "I wonder what's he like?"

For some reason, she had to know.

CHAPTER 1

YOIZUKI AND THE STRONGEST

A GIRL WITH SUNLIGHT AND WIND tangled in her silver hair approached me in front of the Remote Magic Tower and spoke to me. Afterward, she watched me with deep blue eyes that rendered me speechless.

"Amane-san?" she asked, tilting her head at me. "Is something wrong?"

"N-no. Who are you, exactly...?"

"Please call me Claire. We're the same age, so you don't need to speak so formally to me."

"Uh, Claire then."

"Yes, Amane-san."

I might start sweating soon. What was going on here? This conversation was moving too fast and too slow at the same time. Why would she tell me to drop the formalities only to be formal with *my* name? How did she even know my name and age when we'd never met before, anyway? Unless she told me why she came to meet me, this conversation would go nowhere—and I mean nowhere *fast*.

"Do you want something from me...?" I asked, not bothering to hide my wariness. "It sounds like you did a lot of digging to figure out where to meet me."

Her expression scrunched up a little with awkwardness. "I'm sorry. There are reasons for this, I assure you, but I'm sure it's uncomfortable to be investigated in such a way. I understand your displeasure."

"Table the apology for later, okay? What business do you have with me?"

"Thank you for hearing me out. I will respect your time," she said. "I came here today to recruit you into my guild."

"You're a recruiter?"

"Yes. My guild master has spoken to you about joining once before, but you declined. I'm here to renegotiate the terms."

Those were the last words I expected. I looked at her askance. Why would someone go out of their way to scout me *now?* It made sense when I first obtained my unique skill, but once word spread that it was totally useless, the recruiters dried up. I hadn't received a single invite since then.

"Oh, I forgot the most important detail—our guild name," Claire continued, misinterpreting my reservations. "I'm from Yoizuki Guild. Our headquarters is located in this city. Do you know of it?"

"Yoizuki...?"

"Correct."

I rattled the name around in my head until it rang a bell. Over the last few years, it had risen in rank to become the top guild in

Japan. It was one of the few Japanese guilds with some real clout behind it. Wasn't it the guild that Yui had joined? If a prestigious guild like that wanted me, the situation would make even *less* sense.

"Amane-san, I'd like to personally escort you to headquarters to speak with the guild master," Claire said, filling the silence. "Is that acceptable?"

Uncertain, I paused and quickly shuffled the mental card deck options I had at hand. I'd thought about entering a guild—in exchange for the right support—plenty of times. Yoizuki's strength could be worth the tradeoffs. That said, I didn't want to join a guild at this point. I'd have to accept a smorgasbord of limitations and monitoring that I wasn't used to. It was better to focus on leveling up on my own.

Hold on. Saying no is too easy. Something's off about her even asking me about this.

I'd hidden my skills and stats from almost everyone around me (even Hana, until recently). People should see me as a less-than-average adventurer. A top guild like Yoizuki scouting me was even stranger than a small guild...wasn't it? One year was plenty of time for the rumors about my uselessness to reach them. Did they still have hope for my future prospects, even though I turned them down *and* turned out to be weak?

There was too much left unsaid. It might be a good idea to go with her and find out for certain what they knew.

I pulled myself away from the options spread wide in my mind and studied Claire. Something about her nagged at me.

From the moment I saw her, it felt as if something was squirming in my chest—something I couldn't name, though I couldn't bring myself to let go of it.

What an odd feeling. Why? Why did I *want* to chase that feeling?

"Okay," I replied, playing my card of choice. "If you're fine with just a conversation, bring me to your guild."

"Thank you, Amane-san." Claire smiled as she replied. We headed together toward the Yoizuki Guild.

I expected a longer trip, but I followed Claire on a short walk to an idling car on the shoulder of the nearby road instead. The guild must've been located far enough away to require a drive.

"Don't be shy," she said.

"Gotcha."

Claire took the front passenger seat, and I slid into the seat behind her. A man was already sitting in the driver's seat. If I had to guess, he was a member of the Yoizuki guild too. His clothes had the Yoizuki emblem—a moon and a sword—on it.

The man glanced at me. Our eyes met for a moment. Did I imagine the way his eyes narrowed? I hummed in question to myself. I suspected he harbored hostility toward me.

"Yagami-san, please drive," Claire told him.

"Yes, ma'am."

He started the car and pulled out into the road, as instructed.

I must've imagined the hostility. I relaxed into the smooth momentum of the car. No one spoke, so I eventually decided to break the silence.

"Going back to what you said, Claire, did you learn my name and details just for the sake of recruiting me?" I asked.

She was quiet for a beat before answering.

"Yes, I did. Originally, I planned to visit your home, but I saw you on the drive over and approached you at the tower. Thankfully, I didn't miss you. A fortunate miscalculation."

"Right..."

So, that was what she considered a happy accident, huh? Frankly, I was more hung up on the knowledge that this intense girl knew where I lived.

If Claire had the kind of pull to procure personal information, would she know the reason I was being recruited? The guild master would probably tell me once I arrived, but who knew how long this car ride would last? This was a good opportunity.

"Could you tell me something?" I asked.

"Sure. What is it?"

"I expect we'll talk about this soon, but why does Yoizuki want..."

Why does Yoizuki want someone like me?

The whole question never left my mouth. The tangible pressure of a wave of high-density mana washed over us, right from the direction we were headed. It was impossible to ignore. This amount of mana was unheard of outside a dungeon!

"What *was* that?" I asked.

"It must be a dungeon collapse," Claire replied, just as I came to the same conclusion.

A dungeon collapse was a rare phenomenon that occurred before a dungeon destroyed itself. Normally, only adventurers could pass through the Gate of a dungeon above E-rank, but during a pending collapse, monsters could too. That meant monsters could spill into the Return Zone or worse, overflow to the surface. To stop the collapse from causing complete chaos, someone had to dive down and defeat the final boss before it rose to the surface as well.

It was something I had done before, but this time, there was one big problem. I looked to Claire to confirm my hunch.

"Claire, is the dungeon ahead of us the one I think it is?"

"Affirmative, I'm afraid. It's Shiranui, a B-rank dungeon with a level recommendation of 15,000."

"15,000...!"

I'd never stuck a toe inside a dungeon of such high difficulty, let alone beaten one. Not to mention, a dungeon collapse often multiplied the power of its monsters several times over.

While I worried over the danger, Claire twisted in her seat to look back at me.

"Amane-san, we're going to the scene," she said decisively. "We can't get you involved in this. Unfortunately, we'll have to reconvene another day. Is that acceptable?"

"Wait—*you're* going?"

"Correct," she said, as if I'd said the sky was a nice blue today.

She said we were the same age, which made her nineteen years old. How could someone so young be on par with monsters that spawned in a dungeon for a recommended level of *15,000*? Was she backup for Yagami-san? He appeared to be in his late twenties, so it wouldn't be strange if he had that kind of power. But Claire...

Flipping through my options, the most sensible one was leaving and letting Claire and Yagami-san do their thing. Since I lacked experience, there was no guarantee I could handle B-rank monsters, let alone ones stuffed full of mana from a collapse. Besides, they would learn about my true power if I stayed and helped. When I looked at the situation like that, the logical side of brain told me to pick the get-out-of-jail-free card. And yet—

"I'll go too," I said.

"What?" Claire replied.

Instinct pushed back on sense and told me to make a different choice, so I did.

"Amane-san, are you certain? This is a highly unsafe situation," she said. For the first time, Claire sounded uncertain.

"I'm sure. I can help evacuate civilians."

"But..." Her face grew tight and distant as she considered it.

Yagami-san interjected bluntly. "If he wants to come, let him come. He's not a guild member yet, so we can't order him around. Besides, we're already here."

Yagami-san was right; he'd just pulled to a stop in front of Shiranui Dungeon. Adventurers who woke up with plans to face the dungeon were now battling powerful monsters on the surface. From what I could see, they were holding their own—for the time being.

We exited the car and hurried to talk to an adventurer on standby in the rear.

"We're here to assist," Claire said in an authoritative voice. "Tell us what's happening."

The adventurer gave us the quick and dirty: It was taking their full strength to contain the monsters on the surface, and they didn't have a party ready to defeat the final boss yet. During a collapse, it was safest for adventurers at least one rank above the dungeon's usual recommended rank to fight the final boss. They needed an A-rank adventurer—someone level 20,000 or above. Adventurers that powerful weren't growing on trees, so it would take time before one would arrive.

Unfortunately for us, we had run straight into the *worst* possible scenario.

Harsh tremors from within the dungeon shook the ground and knocked us sideways. The last time I felt this sort of tremor, Kenzaki was on the verge of collapse. I swallowed and accepted the truth.

These tremors could only mean one thing.

"*Grooooooaaaaaaaaa!!!*"

An all-consuming roar, almost loud enough to burst our eardrums, pounded into us like a fist. At the same time, the ground above the dungeon split apart. It seemed that Hell itself was opening as a ten-meter-tall monster emerged. Its bulky body bulged with muscles, and its grotesque face bent around one large eye. Club swinging, it charged at us with a strength I sensed was greater than any I'd faced before.

Appraisal confirmed what I instinctually knew.

> **CYCLOPS**
> LEVEL: 40,000

"Level 40,000...!" I gasped.

Even with the numbers swimming in my vision, I couldn't believe it. That level wasn't natural.

I wasn't the only one shocked to see the beast. Fear of an enemy far more powerful than all of us was evident in those around me as they scrambled to retreat.

"Nameless," I said, summoning my favorite weapon from my Item Box. No way could I rely on anything else. I gripped it in both hands and fell into a fighting stance.

Even if people discovered my true strength, I wouldn't regret it if it meant I prevented this monster from killing someone. There was no question—it had to be stopped here and now, and no one else had stepped forward. Nevertheless, I was filled with doubt.

"Can I even do this...?" I muttered to myself.

Such a basic question. Was it possible for *me* to go toe-to-toe with this monster? I'd barely broken level 13,000.

With Nameless and my other stat-boosting skills, my Attack and Speed could rival a level 40,000 monster, but I was incredibly outmatched when it came to everything else. I needed to fight like one hit could kill me.

Another problem, almost as gigantic as the cyclops, loomed in front of me.

We were *outside* of the dungeon.

Dungeon Teleportation only worked if the destination was *inside* a dungeon. Out here, I couldn't activate Time Zero, and that was my best combat skill. That alone was like a skyscraper blocking my path—not to mention I couldn't rely on brute-force attacks against such a massive opponent.

To say I was feeling unprecedented amounts of doom and gloom was no exaggeration.

"But I don't have any other options," I told myself.

I steeled my trembling limbs and set my sights on the beast towering before me. Its one-eyed stare pierced me like an arrow through the chest. It had recognized me as its enemy, ripe for elimination. I raised my sword, about to charge at it, when Claire stepped in front of me.

"Pull back, Amane-san," she said.

"...Huh?"

She coolly turned her head up at the cyclops like she was about to ask it for directions. How were her eyes so calm when the average adventurer had no hope of defeating this creature, even at their apex? I wanted to stop Claire from challenging it, but the words got caught in my throat. I didn't say anything. I *couldn't*. Her valiant stance stole my conviction.

"Cursed," she intoned.

In an instant, a sword manifested in the space before her outstretched right hand. The blade itself was constructed from ice, and it shone a translucent, pale blue. Something of its color seemed to reflect her windswept silver hair.

Everyone's eyes turned away from the cyclops and toward her. Her aura sparked as powerfully as an electromagnet.

Then, before we could blink, Claire *vanished*.

"What?!" I gasped.

Did she teleport? No, that couldn't be it. What she did was far simpler. She moved faster than the naked eye could perceive.

The match was settled before my next pounding heartbeat. Her pale blue sword flashed and carved a neon line in the air, where it sliced the cyclops from bottom to top. Right when the shine of the sword's slash faded, Claire reappeared in midair and flipped elegantly over the cyclops's raised club. She effortlessly stuck her landing behind it.

The cyclops's body wavered left and right, a decrepit tower about to topple to one side. Then, incapable of bearing its weight anymore, the monster split as if halved by heaven itself. Blood should've spilled everywhere, but a crust of ice gleamed over the inside of the cyclops's body, keeping it sealed.

After a few twirls of her sword, Claire strolled back to us.

Instantly, I remembered it.

Everything started to make sense.

"Claire, are you..."

I was so shocked I couldn't finish the sentence, but she must've known what I was thinking, because she just looked at me with those striking, vivid eyes.

The news story circulating—a new celebrity in Japan, the youngest adventurer to make S-rank.

"I didn't inform you about myself besides the fact that I belong to the Yoizuki Guild, did I?" she said. "I'm Kisaragi Claire, S-rank, and currently the twelfth highest level adventurer in Japan."

After Claire's decisive defeat of the cyclops, we helped the other adventurers clear out the remaining monsters on the surface. Some people had taken serious injuries, but luckily, no one was dead—thanks to Claire's immense strength.

No idea what would've happened if I'd fought that monster myself.

Once the cleanup was finished, Claire spoke to the Dungeon Association staff members who arrived on the scene. They didn't look surprised to hear she was the one to defeat the cyclops. Unlike me, Claire didn't hide her abilities from the world. If she did, the news never would have spread that she'd reached S-rank.

After such a brief but amazing show of her might, I wondered: Just how powerful was Claire? At nineteen years old, how could she already be so strong? If I went to Yoizuki, would I learn her secrets? Before I realized it, I was bouncing on the balls of my feet, eagerly anticipating the answer.

Once Claire finished giving her rundown, she returned.

"I apologize for the delay," she said. "Let's be on our way."

For some reason, with Claire back in front of me, I hesitated.

"Amane-san?"

"Uh, right. Let's go."

"One moment. Before that..."

Claire reached down to touch the cyclops. The giant body vanished as if it were never there. Did she fit that hulking thing *inside* her Item Box? How high a level was her skill? Of course she would take it, if she could. As the one who defeated it, she'd earned whatever prize she wanted.

With the cyclops out of the way, we resumed our drive to Yoizuki.

As I climbed out of the car, I inspected the fancy building that stood tall before me. The ostentatious design fit the bill for the HQ of the top guild in Japan.

"My first time at Yoizuki..." I said to myself.

"This way, Amane-san."

"Coming."

I followed Claire inside the building. The hallway was sparkling clean, and as we walked, passersby spoke to Claire in familiar tones.

"Good morning, Claire-san."

"Oh, Claire-chan! Heya!"

"Yes, good morning," she replied.

A lot of the Yoizuki members we passed were in their twenties. How rare. Younger adventurers kept up the hustle and boosted their levels, but most of the *really* good ones were in their thirties and forties. Seeing people close to my age was surprising, as was how they spoke to Claire like she was their friend.

"You sure are popular," I remarked.

"They like me well enough, I suppose, but I think that's more because I'm the daughter of the guild master than anything else."

"You are? I had no idea."

As we spoke, we reached the guild master's office. Claire knocked, and a voice called from inside.

"Enter," he said.

"Please excuse us," Claire said politely as she opened the door. I followed her inside, where an older man sat at a desk heaped with stacks of paper.

Huh. Unexpectedly, I remembered this man from somewhere. Had we met before?

Claire took the lead while I tried to place his face. "I brought Amane-san as you asked. Also, a collapse occurred at Shiranui along the way—"

"That's fine. The Association called me, so no need to report. Well done, Claire." After thanking her, he turned his focus to me. "And thank you for coming, Amane Rin. I'm Yoizuki's guild master, Kisaragi Daisuke. We've met once before when I tried to recruit you. Do you remember me?"

"You tried to recruit me...?" The memory struck. "Oh!"

That was why I remembered him. He was one of the few to approach me about joining a guild after I left the Kings of Unique. At the time, I was burnt out on making friends, so I barely listened to his pitch and turned him down. Definitely the same guy.

Wow, I received a direct invitation from the guild master back then? Dang, that was a shock delayed by a whole year!

"I'll take my leave now," Claire said with a sense of finality. Mission accomplished for her, I supposed. She left us alone in his office without another word.

"Take a seat on that sofa," he suggested. "This isn't a standing conversation."

"...Right."

I obeyed and sat on the tidy guest sofa, feeling uncomfortable as I set my hands on my knees. It was a bit like sitting in the principal's office back in school. He pulled a number of documents off his desk and sat on the opposing sofa.

"Let's jump in, Amane," he said. "Do you have any intention of joining—"

"Before that, can I ask one question?" I interrupted.

It was rude, but he seemed unbothered. He nodded. "Of course. Ask away."

"Why recruit me *now?* Is it like last year, when you saw potential in my unique skill?"

If he had nodded, it would've loosened some of the tension in my shoulders. That was not to be, as he instead smiled cockily and said, "You're partially correct. I do detect value in your unique skill, but..." He paused, as if for dramatic effect. "I have a theory that your potential is no longer a question anymore. I believe you've already awakened to something amazing. To put it bluntly Amane, are you *hiding* your true power?"

His words quickened my pulse. Everything, from what he said to the way he said it, told me he had a solid basis for his belief.

I stayed calm and asked him levelly, "What makes you think that?"

"Is it enough to say the collapse at Kenzaki Dungeon and the Sumifuku Dungeon murder incident convinced me?" he replied.

I kept my mouth shut, but this time, I couldn't hide my unrest as I shifted my legs. I needed to assume he'd uncovered everything. That said, I wasn't going to outright confirm it for him.

"What's your proof?"

"Now, now, don't be hasty. I'll explain everything."

Like a surgeon removing shrapnel, he meticulously pulled out everything about the two incidents that formed his theory: the possibility that I'd entered the boss room during the Kenzaki collapse with Dungeon Teleportation, and the fact I appeared at Sumifuku after I killed Yanagi to save Hana's life. As much as I hated it, his guesses were close to the heart of the truth.

Still, it was just a theory.

"You're assuming I have the power to defeat Kenzaki's final boss *and* Yanagi-san," I countered. "You're aware that my abilities are inferior to those of others my age, aren't you?"

He shook his head. "I don't think that's true anymore. Your teleportation skill was unlike any other. It's possible that it evolved in a direction that changed it into a powerful weapon. Instant teleportation could enable so many things—evasion, closing gaps, or even warping items from long distances. Maybe you could even place Exploding Stones *inside* a monster's body. Regardless, if you were creative, you could defeat much stronger enemies."

I sat there, completely speechless. The part about teleporting items was off, but the part about instant teleportation was spot on. Time Zero had elevated my combat abilities significantly.

Lucky for me, he hadn't realized where Dungeon Teleportation's true worth lay. It was so fantastic, it was hard for even someone like *him* to imagine. My skill's real bread and butter was the ability to bypass the Span—meaning I could dive as much as I wanted.

It sounded like he was far from realizing that, but I didn't want him anywhere close to sniffing things out. So I feigned a *How did you know?* expression to throw him off the scent.

He nodded with satisfaction at busting me. "Ah, it would seem that I'm correct. If you want to hide your power, that's up to you. There was a firestorm around your unique skill when you first got it, but once it proved ineffective, the tables turned. I can imagine why you don't want widespread attention again, even if your skill has improved."

After a brief pause, he continued.

"That's not all you have to think about, is it? Based on what happened at Sumifuku, you had enough power to defeat level 10,000 monsters. That means you've grown at an unusual rate. Now, if *that* got out, trouble would invite itself into your life, like it or not." His expression turned serious. "You can't hide your power forever, which brings me back to my original question. Won't you join Yoizuki? We can offer you support. I think it would be mutually beneficial."

"Support..."

That was what I'd always wanted in order to protect Hana, and to protect myself. This wasn't a *bad* deal. Nonetheless, I couldn't say yes to him so easily.

"Let's say you're right about everything," I said. "That means I'm hiding the fact that I killed Yanagi-san. You sure you want a murderer in your guild?"

"*If* I've guessed correctly, then I know whoever killed Yanagi possesses a strong sense of justice. I also know that other evidence has come to light that implicates Yanagi for a number of cold-blooded crimes," he explained. "Becoming a top adventurer doesn't come without clashes between people, and I welcome anyone who doesn't hesitate to strike in difficult situations."

Clashes between people.

I cast my eyes down at the low table between us. I understood what he meant: For now, our world walked the tightrope of peace, but we were suspended over a chasm echoing with the promise of war. Only twenty years had passed since dungeons spawned around the globe, and life as we knew it was still changing at a frightening speed. Top-class adventurers were as good as military-grade weapons. The more capable adventurers a country had, the more leverage they held on an international scale. Countries with enough adventurers to redraw the world map were regarded as enemies by the others.

The same went for guilds. The competition was on a much smaller scale, but the tension was there. That's exactly why I wanted to hide my power, and why I was tempted by the support and influence of a guild behind me.

But this man—the guild master—was promising Yoizuki could give me that. Is that what I truly wanted?

I hesitated.

Eventually, I lifted my gaze from the table and locked eyes with the guild master. Based on his behavior and the tone of his voice, he didn't seem like a liar. If he was telling the truth, he'd seen my true power and genuinely wanted *me* as a member.

It was time to take a bow and quit my short-lived acting career.

I let out a big sigh, visibly giving up. He'd gathered so much information and confirmed so many facts that I doubted I would convince him otherwise. I nodded in surrender.

"You got it," I admitted. "I defeated the orc general...and I stopped Yanagi."

"Oh? I had you cornered, didn't I? I like a guy who knows when to fold 'em, so to speak," he said. "So, would you like to join my guild? I won't publicize your secrets if you say no. Answer honestly."

"...I'm sorry, but I don't plan to join."

"Why not?"

This was the hitch. Though he knew many of my true capabilities, I didn't want to spill the details about how I became so strong.

"If I join the guild, I'll inevitably have to work with a party," I explained. "I want to keep diving solo."

"Solo? Did your old friends make you distrust new ones?"

"No, no, it's a matter of effectiveness. Dungeon Teleportation only works on me."

"So that's what this is about. You're right, a party might hold you back sometimes. Handling trouble along the way is one thing, but soloing is certainly ideal for targeting specific takedown rewards."

I wasn't lying, but I'd omitted my ability to bypass the Span on purpose. What I'd said was enough reason to turn down his invitation. As much as it hurt to lose potential support, I prioritized boosting my level until it was on par with world-class adventurers over having backup.

The guild master didn't give up so easily. "Think about it. If you form a party, you can challenge dungeon bosses that you can't handle on your own. That would increase your takedown rewards and help your growth long-term. Are you really sure about letting that opportunity go?"

"Well..."

The guild master wasn't wrong. I liked to plan ahead, and his own forward-thinking made it even harder to refuse. Sensing he had a chance to sway me, he continued with a suggestion.

"Why don't you join on a provisional basis?"

"You mean joining...temporarily?"

He nodded and spread his arms wide open, though his face was serious. "Consider it a test period for the compatibility between adventurer and guild! I don't mind if you continue soloing. In exchange, would you like to dive with a high-rank adventurer once or twice?"

A high-rank adventurer—the silver-haired Claire immediately sprang to mind. If she joined me with her shiny S-rank classification, I'd have no complaints. Not to mention, I might glimpse how she reached her abnormal strength if I formed a party with her.

Okay, I was interested, but there *had* to be a catch.

"That's not a bad deal, but what if other people learn what I can do? I don't want to share that unless I officially join," I said.

"I'll place a gag order on those who form a party with you," the guild master countered. "We take secrets very seriously, I assure you, but if you don't trust us then there's nothing more I can offer you. How about it, Amane Rin?"

The deal was on the table between us, so to speak. On the one hand, I would risk my secret getting out, but on the other hand, I might gain knowledge, growth, and support. As long as they didn't interfere with my solo activities, would it hurt to try out membership? After some thought, I made my decision.

"Okay," I said. "I'll join on a provisional basis."

"Great decision."

For the first time, his deal-making face softened into a smile. He truly seemed glad that I'd decided to try out the guild. I wasn't sure *why* he was that happy about it, but I thought it would be weird if I asked, so I didn't.

We spent some time discussing the terms, conditions, and future plans of my provisionary membership. Finally, we exchanged contact information and I left his office. With my business over, I planned to head home.

"Rin?" said a familiar voice.

"Rin-senpai, what're you doing here?" said another.

"Huh?"

I turned, and my eyes widened as I took in the two familiar faces. Kurosaki Rei and Kasai Yui stood in front of me.

"Hey, Rei. *And* Yui," I said awkwardly.

A few minutes after I joined Yoizuki—temporarily, at least—in the guild master's office, I found myself in one of the building's standby rooms.

"How did this happen...?" I murmured without meaning to.

The room had a furnished space to eat, where I now sat at a table with Rei and Yui—*and* Claire, who somehow felt the most unexpected, even though she was the person who brought me to Yoizuki.

"Something wrong?" Claire asked from the seat to my left.

"It's nothing," I replied in a hurry. But, seriously, wasn't it strange for her to join us so casually?

As surprised as I was to see Rei and Yui in Yoizuki (especially Rei), they were pretty surprised to see me too. Apparently, Claire was giving them a tour and they were on the way to this very room when we ran into each other.

Okay, so the *how* of it was simple, but I was still hung up on the *why*. Was fate setting me up?

Rei and Yui wanted to know why I was at Yoizuki too, of course. I told them about my decision to join on a provisional basis, and we decided to chat about what we'd been up to lately.

A guild clerk brought over two small plates of snacks and hot tea for everyone.

"Here you go," she said.

"Thank you."

I accepted them with a grateful nod, but internally, I was squirming. Other people were sitting around the room and many of them had turned to watch us. Maybe because I was a newcomer, or because of Claire?

I told myself I shouldn't take it to heart.

Instead, I pushed the conversation forward. "I didn't expect you to join Yoizuki, Rei."

"There were limits to going solo," she said.

The world sure was a small place. I never imagined Rei would join Yoizuki of all guilds. Maybe Yui invited her, or the guild master set his sights on her because of her unique skill. Either way, she must've liked the energy of Yoizuki if she'd decided to join.

In the seat diagonal from mine, Yui smiled. "I was more surprised to see *you* here, Rin-senpai! What changed your mind?"

"A few things."

"Well, whatever the reason, I'm so glad you joined!"

"Yeah, uh, I'll...make the best of it." It was kind of embarrassing to be the reason for her obvious joy.

Beside me, Claire nodded with interest. "You two seem rather close. I heard you were about two years apart?"

"Well, the thing is," Yui chirped in her bright, chatty voice, "when I only just became an adventurer, Rin-senpai rescued me from a super dangerous situation! After that, I found out his little sister was my kouhai at school. That's why we're *so* close now."

"I see. Is he the senpai you said you look up to?"

"The senpai you look up to...?" I echoed.

"C-Claire-senpai!" Yui blushed and waved her hands as if to dispel Claire's words. "You don't need to bring that up..."

Based on Yui's outsized reaction, what Claire said was true. I was surprised to hear that Yui was talking me up around the guild, but hey. Not a bad feeling.

"Yui, you can have this," I said, sliding a snack plate toward her as thanks.

"Huh? Uh, thank you...?"

Rei's neutral expression furrowed downward into a frown. "Why only Yui? I can sing your praises as well as she can..."

I didn't know what set her off, but clearly Rei was feeling competitive. What followed was a barrage—she rapid-fired compliments at me for three whole minutes without running out of ammo.

"Okay, okay!" I interjected. "That's plenty."

To quiet her down, I plucked a toothpick with one of the snacks from the second plate and handed it to her. She stuffed it in her mouth and chewed haughtily, but I could tell she was pleased. She was like a small animal who needed a treat. It was cute.

Completely by accident, I'd given away all of my snacks, but that was okay.

"Rin-senpai, you didn't eat any of them. Are you okay with that?" Yui asked, reading my mind.

I didn't want to make her feel guilty, so I grasped for a reason it was fine.

"Nah, I'm on a diet right now," I fibbed.

The air around us froze. Yui and Rei looked at each other and simultaneously pushed the plate with the last snack back to the middle of the table.

"Well, *I* like watching you enjoy snacks," Yui huffed. "So have at it!"

"As did I," Rei added.

"O-oh. Okay?"

My excuse only increased the pressure on me, somehow. Since they'd outvoted me, I moved the plate back and ended up right where the conversation started.

I turned to Claire, who was also giving off a powerful aura, even greater than the other girls. She touched the final snack plate, glanced between the plate and me several times, then slid it over to herself.

"...Eat it now or *I* will," she said.

She looked so calm that I didn't expect a reaction like that from her. I was speechless under her level gaze. In a rush, I stuffed the snack in my mouth to hide the wobbly feeling that she gave me.

"Thanks," I said after I washed it down with the somewhat-cooled tea. I finally felt like I could take a full breath.

We talked for a while longer. I felt like I knew them all a little better by the end of it.

CHAPTER 2

EXPLOSIVE SPEED LEVELING

A FEW DAYS AFTER the events at Yoizuki headquarters, I traveled to a new C-rank dungeon called Kuze. Before heading inside, I stopped in front of it and double-checked my Dungeon Teleportation skill.

DUNGEON TELEPORTATION LV 20

REQUIRED MP: 1 MP × Distance (meters)

CONDITIONS: Teleportation can only occur in dungeons that have already been visited.

TELEPORTATION DISTANCE: Maximum 400 meters.

ACTIVATION TIME: 0.8 seconds × distance (meters)

SCOPE: User and user's belongings.

SUB-SKILL: Time Zero

Paying 100 MP allows the user to teleport instantly within a ten-meter radius. (This ability is obtained when Dungeon Teleportation reaches LV 20).

Like the description said, I couldn't enter dungeons I'd never stepped inside of. I'd entered tons of C-rank dungeons—without beating them—to make the most of this ability. I still had a good number of them left to explore, including this one.

"Time to go," I said. "Dungeon Teleportation."

I reappeared inside Kuze. With a recommended level of 800, it was one of the less difficult C-rank dungeons. It surpassed Kenzaki—home of the Nameless Knight—but wasn't quite as difficult as Marou, where I fought the Rainbow King Wolf. Although, the Nameless Knight was level 1,100...hmm, maybe Kenzaki had more substance to it than I was giving it credit for.

Kobolds and golems spawned along my way, drawing me out of my memories. I'd only run Kuze once, just to check out the interior, but now, I was over level 13,000. I didn't need to tread carefully, like I did back then.

"I'm gonna crush this!" I declared. "Dungeon Teleportation."

I used my skill to drop straight to the last floor. Was my experience at the Remote Magic Tower the reason I could proceed so confidently? It was strange to feel like a new version of myself.

"No sense dwelling. Time to challenge the boss."

Once I entered the boss room, a level 800 ice golem charged at me. Its dense, glacial body deflected my blade, but our levels were about as far apart as the moon is from the stars. Greed cut it down in a single hit.

"You have defeated the dungeon boss."

"Gained XP: Level increased by 12!"

"Nice. First run down, a bunch more to go. I'm just getting started!"

It seemed like forever since I looped a dungeon. Holding onto that motivated feeling, I beat the dungeon as many times as the day allowed.

The next day, on my sixtieth dungeon win, the system spoke in my mind.

"You have reached this dungeon's maximum number of allotted victories."

"Bonus Reward: Level increased by 30!"

"You will no longer receive rewards for defeating this dungeon."

"Oh! Finally maxed it out."

That made it my eleventh dungeon fully traveled. What happened to my Dungeon Traveler title when I surpassed ten? Curiosity compelled me to open the stats display.

> **DUNGEON TRAVELER (10/10)**
> A title granted to someone who has traversed a dungeon in its entirety.
> By traveling a dungeon a specific number of times, this person gains special benefits.

"Still ten out of ten... Does that mean I won't gain any extra special rewards?"

Huh. That didn't bode well.

If maxing out twenty dungeons wasn't my ticket to accessing the Remote Magic Tower again, I'd never figure out what that mysterious third reward was. Had that ship really sailed for good? To be honest, I felt shell-shocked.

Ugh, this sucks...

Never was one for sulking though. Since it didn't seem like I could muscle my way back into the Remote Magic Tower, I would let that third reward go. *For now.*

"At least I earned some SP. How should I use all of it?" I wondered.

I checked my stats again.

AMANE RIN

LEVEL: 14,367   SP: 16,210

TITLES: Dungeon Traveler (10/10), Nameless Swordsman,
    Endbringer (ERROR), Wiser Wise Man

HP: 112,100/112,100   MP: 17,330/31,570

ATTACK: 26,870   DEFENSE: 22,630   SPEED: 28,100

INTELLIGENCE: 22,290   RESISTANCE: 22,430   LUCK: 21,350

SKILLS: Dungeon Teleportation LV 20, Enhanced Strength LV MAX,
    Herculean Strength LV MAX, Superhuman Strength LV MAX,
    High-speed Movement LV MAX, Gale Wind LV MAX,
    Revitalize LV 1, Purification Magic LV 1, Mana Boost LV MAX,
    Mana Recovery LV 2, Enemy Detection LV 4, Evasion LV 4,
    Status Condition Resistance LV 4, Appraisal, Item Box LV 5,
    Conceal LV 1, Battle Barrier LV 1, Plunderer LV 1

I had a veritable treasure trove of SP saved up—16,210 points in total. A hefty sum, but how best to spend it?

"Let's see which skills would serve my future plans best," I mumbled, darting my eyes over the ones that jumped out.

OBTAINED SKILLS

Dungeon Teleportation LV 20 → LV 21 (SP NEEDED: 10,000)

Battle Barrier LV 1 → LV 2 (SP NEEDED: 10,000)

Status Condition Resistance LV 4 → LV 5 (SP NEEDED: 1,000)

Enemy Detection LV 4 → LV 5 (SP NEEDED: 1,000)

Evasion LV 4 → LV 5 (SP NEEDED: 1,000)

Item Box LV 5 → LV 6 (SP NEEDED: 1,200)

NEW SKILLS

Endurance LV 1 (SP NEEDED: 100)

Enhanced Mana LV 1 (SP NEEDED: 100)

Enhanced Spirit LV 1 (SP NEEDED: 100)

Etc.

"That's the gist, huh?"

I considered my options. First were the new skills: Endurance, Enhanced Mana, and Enhanced Spirit. They would boost my Defense, Intelligence, and Resistance, respectively. It was easiest to think of them as similar to Herculean Strength and High-speed Movement, but for different stats.

"As much as I want to spend what I've saved up, it would take a ton of SP to even notice a difference. I should preserve my points for now."

Getting any of these skills to LV 10 would only boost my stats by 3,000 points. These were the kind of skills people obtained just to unlock the ones above them. There were better options.

I turned my attention to my obtained skills. Most of them were hungry for a *big* heapin' helping of points. Still, this would be a difficult decision. The only ones that weren't quite as voracious were these four: Status Condition Resistance, Enemy Detection, Evasion, and Item Box.

"If I'm picking something geared toward high-difficulty dungeons instead of speed runs, should I prioritize Item Box?" I wondered.

At LV 1, Item Box was basically a glorified backpack. Leveling it up increased the capacity exponentially. Now that it was level five, it fit my weapons, magic stones, monster corpses, and other miscellaneous items, but it might help to create some wiggle room moving forward. My future likely held a plethora of bulky, valuable monster corpses—ones like the cyclops that Claire bagged at Shiranui.

"Okay, I'll start with Item Box. But what should I do with *these* two skills?" My attention slid back to two hungriest skills on the list. "Dungeon Teleportation and Battle Barrier...maybe I'll boost one of them."

Both of them required 10,000 SP to level up, but they were worth it so I didn't have any complaints on that front. I selected Battle Barrier to freshen my memory of the description.

BATTLE BARRIER LV 1

Until MP is fully depleted, this skill creates a mana barrier around
the target. (The strength and duration of the effect changes
according to skill level.)

COOLDOWN TIME: 60 seconds

"'Strength and duration of the effect changes according to skill level,'" I read. "That's important."

Battle Barrier was massively useful during my fight with Yanagi. It protected me from his daggers several times. The caveat was that his level was barely 10,000 and his fighting style was based on speed, not strength. He didn't have a lot of power in his hits. Even someone like him could've broken through the barrier with a few dozen hits, which meant keeping Battle Barrier at LV 1 might not help me much in battles with stronger enemies. I had to level it up at *some* point.

That didn't mean I had to do it now, though!

"Yeah, it's not super strong, but that means I don't need to touch the skill level until I plan to face an opponent stronger than Yanagi," I decided. "I'll stick with grinding safe dungeons for a while."

That left one candidate: my unique skill, Dungeon Teleportation.

"The SP required to level it up this time is *way* higher than it was. It probably won't feel different until LV 30, but I can test it and see whether it's worth pushing the skill level higher in the long term."

"Dungeon Teleportation has increased to LV 21."

"Conditions have changed."

"Teleportation can only occur in dungeons that have already been visited → Teleportation can occur in all dungeons."

"Wha—?!" I blurted.

I choked on the word in my astonishment, and could anyone blame me?

"All dungeons? This means I don't have to tap in and out of new dungeons to avoid the Span. Heck, I don't have to worry about the Span *at all*. This is wild...!" I marveled. "The teleportation distance hasn't changed so it doesn't help me with the Remote Magic Tower, but even without that...wow. This is freakin' *huge*."

I'd considered how to incorporate new B-level dungeons into my routine, since they were more suited to my level, but this development eliminated the need to figure out logistics. I could enter whatever dungeon I wanted, *whenever* I wanted.

"This is giving me a major tailwind!" I said excitedly. I would level up faster *and* easier, all thanks to this.

With a spring in my step and the winds behind me, I invested my remaining SP into boosting Item Box to LV 6 and headed home.

DUNGEON TELEPORTATION LV 21

REQUIRED MP: 1 MP × Distance (meters)

CONDITIONS: Teleportation can occur in all dungeons.

TELEPORTATION DISTANCE: Maximum 400 meters.

ACTIVATION TIME: 0.8 seconds × distance (meters)
SCOPE: User and user's belongings.

SUB-SKILL: Time Zero
Paying 100 MP allows the user to teleport instantly within a
    ten-meter radius. (This ability is obtained when Dungeon
    Teleportation reaches LV 20.)

The day after I completed Kuze and raised Dungeon Teleportation to LV 21, the world was my oyster—to open with my sword, of course! The Span no longer had its claws in me, so I could've challenged a new dungeon—like one of the B-rank dungeons with a recommended level of 10,000 or above I'd been eyeing. But I didn't do that. Instead, I went back to a dungeon I already maxed out—the C-rank dungeon, Niimi.

Hana stood beside me in front of the Gate. I squeezed her hand protectively.

"You okay?"

"Yeah," she replied. "Better than I expected."

Seeing her smile, I didn't think she was covering. I would understand if dungeons were a sore spot for her after everything that happened, but she seemed all right.

"Want to head in?" I asked.

"Let's do it!"

Together, we stepped inside Niimi's depths.

Hana told me about what happened with Yanagi directly after our death match, but outside of the heat of the moment, we went over the details of what happened again. That conversation brought my attention to an intriguing detail.

Yanagi rigged a situation where Hana had to defeat a strong monster just so he could confirm the value of her unique skill, Stock. The monster's defeat boosted her level exponentially. When she showed me her stats display, this was what it said:

AMANE HANA

LEVEL: 521   **SP:** 4,750

HP: 3,820/3,820   **MP:** 1,390/1,390

ATTACK: 820   **DEFENSE:** 900   **SPEED:** 820

INTELLIGENCE: 940   **RESISTANCE:** 820   **LUCK:** 820

SKILLS: Stock LV 1, Enhanced Strength LV 3, Mana Manipulation LV 3, Mana Boost LV 5.

STOCK LV 1

CONDITIONS: Directly touching a target copies their skill, so long as it is LV 1 or below.

COPY CAPACITY: Maximum one skill.

COPY DURATION: Maximum ten minutes (touching the target again lengthens the effects).

The first time I saw the scope of her growth, it shocked me. A whole year of leveling only got me to level 200, but she'd surpassed it with one win. That much growth within a few days of obtaining her stats surely put her among the fastest levelers in the world. The question now was how she would use those new levels, stats, and SP.

Hana said she wanted the power to protect herself *and* other people—and I wanted to help her achieve her dreams. That was why I brought her to this dungeon. There was no better battle advice than that given while in action.

"This spot should be good," I said after confirming this floor (the second) was clear of adventurers. "How about we get started?"

"I'm ready!"

First, she needed to decide how to spend her SP pool. We stood together and read over her display screen, checking how much SP each skill level required.

> **OBTAINED SKILLS**
> Stock LV 1 → LV 2 (SP NEEDED: 1,000)
> Enhanced Strength LV 3 → LV 4 (SP NEEDED: 40)
> Mana Manipulation LV 3 → LV 4 (SP NEEDED: 800)
> Mana Boost LV 5 → LV 6 (SP NEEDED: 1,200)

Every skill but Enhanced Strength required a huge investment to bump it up to the next level. Stock was particularly expensive, ringing in at a shocking 1,000 SP to boost it to LV 2. Considering how promising the skill was, the high cost was a given, but it still felt like a gut punch.

Hana turned to me. "Oniichan, which skills do I need?"

"Honestly? All of them."

The unique skill was the obvious front-runner, but Hana's other skills were highly versatile and stood on their own. That was my professional brotherly opinion, at least. Mana Manipulation would make mana much easier to handle when casting spells, for example. It was a technique-enhancing skill along the lines of Swordsmanship or Spearmanship, but for mana. Manamanship? No, that sounded stupid. Anyway, it was perfect for increasing the base damage behind magic attacks and improving the adventurer's agility with them.

Basically, it increased mastery.

I reined in my galloping thoughts and refocused on which skill she needed to choose *today*. The answer jumped right out at me.

"You've got plenty of SP to play with, so start by boosting Enhanced Strength to LV 10. That'll open up three stat-boosting skills called Herculean Strength, Endurance, and High-speed Movement. They'll help you make the most out of Stock and give you some wiggle room in close combat."

"All righty then, I'll go with that."

Hana trusted me from the bottom of her heart, so she boosted Enhanced Strength to LV 10 without hesitation, for a total cost of 490 SP.

Next would be the *real* game changer.

"Let's address Stock," I said. "You know this skill is the key to becoming a strong adventurer, right?"

"I know, oniichan. If I learn how to use it, it could help me beat much stronger opponents than me," she replied attentively.

"Exactly. The caveat that you can only copy skills at LV 1 is too limiting to be useful, realistically. If possible, you should aim to copy skills as high as LV 5."

"So I gotta level up Stock as much as I can?"

"Yeah. Try boosting it to LV 2 first to get a feel for the kind of change it'll give."

"Okay." Hana boosted Stock to LV 2.

With a flicker, the description on her display changed.

STOCK LV 2

CONDITIONS: Directly touching a target copies their skill, so long as it is LV 2 or below.
COPY CAPACITY: Maximum 2 skills.
COPY DURATION: Maximum 20 minutes (touching the target again lengthens the effects).

"So, this is the kind of change it yields..." I mused.

The maximum skill level Hana could copy elevated to LV 2, and her copied skill capacity increased to two as well. Plus, the duration changed to twenty minutes! She won the jackpot when it came to skill leveling.

"Oniichan, is this a good or bad thing?" she asked.

"It's great. Better than great! You're gonna get some solid milage with this."

"Really?!"

Hana beamed from ear to ear. Call me corny, but her smile made me melt inside.

We decided she should elevate Stock to LV 3 and save the remaining SP for later. We'd figure out next steps after I saw her fight with my own eyes.

With the both of us fired up, we set off to find a monster for her to eliminate.

Five minutes or so later, Hana and I bumped into a small, yellow, demon-like creature with a large club—a goblin. Appraisal showed it was level 400. For a battle novice like Hana, it was a high-level opponent; but from a stats standpoint, she was in the clear. Worst-case scenario, I was prepared to sweep in with an emergency big brother maneuver to rescue her.

Hana paled with nervousness as the goblin approached.

"You got this?" I asked gently.

"Yeah." She nodded and swallowed. "I can do it."

She evaluated the goblin from a distance with two skills she'd borrowed from me, stocked up and ready to go: Battle Barrier LV 1 and Mana Recovery LV 2. Battle Barrier was a battle skill, but since it was a defensive skill, she had to use a different method to attack. Instead of magic, she wielded a short sword I brought for her. It suited her current level, so she shouldn't struggle to damage the goblin.

"Here I go!" she said.

"Grr!"

The not-so-epic fight began. The level difference, boosted

skill parameters, and Hana's athletic abilities all fed into her immediate advantage. The goblin swung its club, but it was clumsy and missed. She took advantage of the opportunity to strike it several times with the short sword. Gradually, her uncertain hits sapped the goblin's health, sending it closer to zero.

She's on the path to victory, I thought to myself. I relaxed, until the goblin snarled and surprised both of us. Instead of swinging the club like I'd expect, it flung it at her. Hana—shocked that it would abandon its only weapon—rushed to block with the short sword, but the momentum of the club knocked the sword out of her hand.

The goblin lurched forward, seizing on its lucky opening. It closed the distance faster than Hana could respond, picked up its club, and swung at her.

If this keeps up, she could get hurt. Even with Battle Barrier, there was still risk involved. I stepped forward.

"Huh?"

Hana's response stopped me in my tracks.

"You're a real pain!" she shouted.

Faster than the crude beast could swing, she punched it in the face with the full weight of her body, and heck, her form was crisp too! The punch sent the squealing goblin tumbling like a tied-off sock full of coins.

"Uh... well, then."

I didn't know how to react. Here I thought she'd resort to magic to take it down. Who would have predicted sweet Hana using her fists instead? The difference in stats and the flow of new strength moving through her must've inspired her. She handled it like a pro.

The goblin landed flat on its back, defenseless. She darted over to her short sword, tightened her grip, and brought it down for a merciless finishing blow. Then she whirled to face me.

"I won, oniichan!"

"C-congrats."

I'd worried that the trauma from Yanagi would hold her back, but she swept right past my fears. She won like a champ—that wasn't easy for a novice to pull off!

Could my little sister really have nerves this steely? When I thought about it, she *was* only level 2 when she defeated that level 10,000 treant. She acted because her life was in danger, but it still took a lot of bravery.

Once she got her celebrating out of her system, I checked in with her.

"Did you get hurt punching the goblin with your bare fist?" Even just a scratch could turn into a problem later.

"Nope, I'm good," Hana said. "I used Battle Barrier to cut the damage to zero."

"Huh. I never thought of using it that way."

It made sense; if the barrier protected her from taking a hit, it could protect Hana from injury when walloping a goblin. I'd only ever used it as a form of defense, but Hana immediately thought to use it as a brace for her fist. Maybe she had a natural talent for quick thinking too. Like brother, like sister, I guess?

If she could use Stock to copy powerful skills and use them in creative ways, just how amazing an adventurer would she become?

Hmm. Unlike me, Hana could only perform her best if she

joined a party. She needed allies with solid skills to make the most of Stock's potential. It wasn't a stretch to say that her strength and fighting methods would depend entirely on the circumstances around her. Joining one specific party might hold her back. A guild was her best bet. If possible, I wanted her to join the same guild as me—in my heart, it was a must.

Since I was testing out Yoizuki, that was the clear candidate. They were a top guild and very selective, but if we revealed her talent, I was sure they'd recruit her without hesitation. Unfortunately, whether we could trust them with her secret was another matter entirely.

"Why'd you go quiet, oniichan?" Hana asked.

"Oh, it's nothing."

I dipped my chin and placed a hand gently on Hana's head to relax her. I did a lot of hypothesizing, but ultimately, which guild she joined was her decision. In the meantime, I would do what I could to help her.

"Sorry for spacing out. If you think you're ready, want to find your next monster?"

"Yeah!"

We spent the next hour hiking around the dungeon. Hana gained confidence with every monster she fought, but she started to wear out too. Once she began to waver from fatigue, I decided we should call it quits for the day.

On second thought, stopping altogether wasn't the most effective way for her to level up. She was a high school student, and since she still had to attend class, she only dived once or twice a week. That wasn't much different than the effects of the Span.

As Hana walked by my side, I continued to mull things over. If the Span wasn't a concern, she should at least beat the dungeon before we went home...but Dungeon Teleportation only worked on me. With our current pace, it would take us nearly half the day to reach the boss level. I doubted she had the stamina for that.

After much silent deliberation, I concluded there was only one way to handle this.

"Let's keep going!" I exclaimed.

"What?!"

I grabbed her in a princess carry and dashed at full clip toward the last floor. Thirty minutes later, she knocked out the boss with one solid punch and grew by twelve levels.

I paid the price for that stunt.

Outside the dungeon, Hana glared at me. I knew she was mad, but the way her cheeks puffed up was downright precious.

"Oniichan?" she said.

"Yes?" I braced myself.

"You could've just said, 'Hey Hana, we should complete the dive. I have a great idea how to get there. Mind if I try?' or *something* like that!" she shouted. "You didn't have to hoist me like a sack of potatoes and take off at high-speed! I mean, it was kinda fun, but still!"

She had fun? Well, if she admitted that, she couldn't be *too* angry.

"You did it *for* me, so I'll forgive you." She let out a prolonged sigh and offered her hand. "As repayment, you have to hold my hand as we go home."

"Sure."

I didn't mind once bit: I held her hand all the way home.

It was barely past noon and too soon for me to quit, so after we grabbed a quick lunch, I left Hana to rest at home. I set out for a dungeon on my own again—a new one, this time.

I noticed tons of geared-up adventurers around me as I reached it. Based on their equipment, they were seasoned fighters. They had to be to challenge this particular dungeon. It was called Suzuka: a B-rank dungeon with a recommended level of 10,000. With the way takedown rewards worked, the higher the person's level, the more effective they were at leveling up, but that didn't make it easy. For most people, it took a minimum of five or six years to reach level 10,000.

These adventurers invested *so* much time into dives. Their aura was light-years apart compared to C-rank-or-lower adventurers.

"It finally feels like I'm one of them," I whispered. "Yes!"

I centered myself and headed toward Suzuka's entrance. Now that Dungeon Teleportation was LV 21, I could enter even though I'd never stepped foot inside this dungeon. With my new power, the Span couldn't influence my actions *at all*.

"Dungeon Teleportation."

This was it. My first B-rank dungeon.

The higher the difficulty, the more levels a dungeon had, and B-rank dungeons were no exception. Something about the formation of a dungeon meant it expanded outward as it spiraled deeper into the earth. The deeper the dungeon, the wider. Suzuka had a whopping fifty floors, and each one stretched for kilometers. It was so vast, it could take days to beat if I didn't optimize my strategy.

Of course, I didn't tackle the dungeon like a normal adventurer!

"It's only been a few minutes, but I'm over halfway through!" I marveled, realizing just how far Dungeon Teleportation had taken me. I was on the thirtieth floor, which would've taken hours for other adventurers.

I was about to stop patting myself on the back and teleport to the thirty-first floor when I heard a loud, feral hiss. A skittering sound followed, drawing closer. My body shouted *evade*. I dodged just in time for something red to rush past me. With a whooshing sound, it zoomed back to where it came from.

I followed the motion of it with my eyes and saw it halt. Once it was still, I could take in that it was a large lizard with stony scales. I used Appraisal on it for the full story.

> **ROCK LIZARD**
> LEVEL: 8,000
> A lizard-type monster with scales made of rocks. The tough scales can repel blade and magic attacks.

"A level 8,000 rock lizard wants a piece of me, hm?"

Luck kept me from encountering any monsters thus far, but luck always ran out eventually. Time Zero was an option to side-step it and beeline for the next floor, but something told me to stand my ground.

"Might as well fight it since I'm here."

There came a point when a boss-battle-only diet was detrimental to my fighting experience. If an enemy wanted aggro, I would give it aggro in spades.

"Greed," I commanded. The glittering short sword manifested from my Item Box.

Blade attacks weren't the most effective against this monster, but it didn't hurt to try. Besides, I had one other trick up my sleeve.

> **NAMELESS SWORDSMAN**
> A title given to someone who relied solely on their blade and their own strength to overcome a difficult enemy.

> When the owner of this title levels up, the equipped bladed
> weapon also gains extra features.
> If the owner of this title possesses skills related to bladed
> weapons, the effects of this title will not manifest.

It was important to mix things up and let Nameless Swordsman affect my best weapons. Equipping Greed gave me exactly that.

"Here we go."

I took a breath and burst toward the rock lizard. It hissed at my approach and fired its sharp spear of a tongue at me. It was so close, damage was unavoidable—but not for me!

"You're late."

At my level, attacks like this were no surprise. I swiftly stepped sideways and swung Greed. The lizard's angry screech was cut short as I severed its tongue with one hit. Time for offense!

"Haaa!"

I couldn't hack at the scales like an unskilled butcher. I had to aim for the space *between* them and cleave away with sharp, pointed attacks. My strategy paid off as my pinpoint blows cut deeply into its body and hewed the scales off. They went flying like debris off a gravel truck. My next goal was to target the exposed flesh. Unfortunately, a rock lizard wouldn't go down that easily.

It spat another hiss and the remaining scales burst off its body as if a bomb had gone off inside it. Dozens of heavy scales came flying at me.

"Time Zero!" I shouted. I warped away from it in an instant, narrowly evading the attack. *That* was out of left field, but the lizard was naked without armor to protect it. One precision attack would kill it.

"...Oh?"

All at once, new scales sprouted across the lizard's body, restoring its pebbly hide.

"Regeneration powers! Though maybe 'regeneration' is too generous, assuming the internal damage remains...not that it matters. If the scales grow back, I just need a new strategy."

I returned Greed to Item Box and lightly punched my left palm with my right fist, raring for a fight. The sound of fabric on fabric was cathartic.

"If it can recover after losing its scales, lemme see how it likes a nice, firm punch," I said. "Battle Barrier!"

The invisible barrier cloaked me. I used Time Zero again and reappeared above the rock lizard, where I shouted, "Take this!"

Fist-first, I collided with the lizard.

WISER WISE MAN
A title granted to those who complete the quest Wise Man's War
under particular conditions.
Grants 50% parameter increase to Attack, Defense, and Speed
when no weapon is equipped.

With Wiser Wise Man powering my fists, the scales cracked and crumbled as I pummeled it, opening the lizard up like a juicy can of fish I could tear into.

"Yes!" I said after it finally collapsed. "I earned that win."

After nudging it once more to confirm it wouldn't regenerate, I collected its magic stone and continued my dive.

I didn't encounter any monsters after my fight with the rock lizard, so I found myself on the final floor in no time. The boss room door towered above me, stark and unfeeling.

"Wow, not even thirty minutes to get down here. It feels kind of like cheating to tackle my first B-rank dungeon so easily, but who's going to complain, I guess." I took a deep breath. "Time to shake it off and get it over with."

On that note, I opened the massive doors with a bold push. They swung open to reveal an empty room with a flame-draped lizard in the center.

A salamander.

I walked in, sizing the beast up as the doors shut behind me. The salamander was large—at least a meter tall. I admit, I researched this dungeon to find out what kind of boss I was in for ahead of time, but...just in case, I used Appraisal.

SALAMANDER

LEVEL: 10,000

A monster clad in fierce flame. It can manipulate fire at will and land strong attacks with its tough body.

"Sounds like what I read. I should be fine."

I equipped Greed and faced the salamander, but it moved first. It roared so loud that the space around us shook. As if the roar was a spell, fire gathered in front of its mouth in the shape of a long lance. It narrowed its gleaming black eyes and launched the scorching-hot spear of flame my way. If it hit me, I'd take massive damage.

Big *if.*

"Absorb it, Greed!" As the fire touched the transparent gleam of my blade, it was sucked into it. The blade lit up with a crimson color. "Ha, how you like *that?*"

The salamander wasn't a clever creature. It froze in bewilderment upon seeing this turn of events, and I didn't let the opening go. No need for Time Zero. In a flash, I activated my speed-boosting skills and closed in on the salamander.

I slashed at its magma-covered, slick body in a flurry of attacks—but then I wondered something. What if Greed could absorb the fire that cloaked the salamander's body? If it could absorb a monster's water and lightning attacks, a magic cloak shouldn't be impossible. This was a good chance to experiment.

"Absorb!"

The blade ravenously absorbed the weaving flames and exposed the salamander's wet body to the air, completely removing its only armor.

"It worked!" I exclaimed.

Unlike the rock lizard, it didn't have hard stone scales to hide behind. I brought my blade down and struck deep. It screeched and bucked with no regard for the blade slicing its flesh, propelling me and Greed backward with the force of its thrashing.

"Whoa!"

Not the kind of enemy that would die easily with one hit, huh? But the odds were still very much in my favor.

"Hyaaa!" I held Greed with both hands and chopped into the salamander's face. It shrieked as liquid filled its ruined mouth, but there was no more fight left in it. It slumped to the floor moments later.

The system spoke in my head.

"You have defeated the dungeon boss."

"Gained XP: Level increased by 1!"

"Dungeon Takedown Reward: Level increased by 50!"

"Woo! I beat the dungeon!" I cheered. For my first B-rank dungeon, this was way easier than I expected, but that checked out considering my high level.

"Phew. It's good I managed to absorb its cloak, but that cost a lot of MP."

The MP bar in the corner of my vision had reduced by a quarter. Most of that was from absorbing the salamander's armor. It was a stark indicator of how much mana a boss like the salamander had to play with. The lightning beast's armor was the same way; it had enough mana to maintain it *and* restore the armor when it broke. Depending on the monster, this could make a great trick, but I needed to time when I used it.

Enough thinking! I needed to gather the magic stone and return to the surface with my takedown reward. Supposedly, Suzuka's takedown reward was a magic item called a Mana

Amplification Stone. Like other magic stones, it came infused with mana, but a Mana Amplification Stone worked as a *source* of magic energy for adventurers—and an excellent one at that. When a spell was released, the stone's mana could boost its power exponentially. They were popular among sorcerers, so it would fetch a good price.

I waited on tenterhooks for my reward to manifest, but...

"Is the system asleep?" I complained. No matter how long I waited, there was no sign of it. It should've dropped into my inventory by now.

"Wait a minute. I feel like this happened bef—"

"First-time challenger of this dungeon: Confirmed."

"Solo dungeon takedown: Confirmed."

"Dungeon defeated within sixty minutes of entry: Confirmed."

"Condition of 'Hunter of Divine Speed': Fulfilled."

"Now spawning extra boss: Gryphon."

"I *knew* it!!!" I hollered.

Abruptly, the sound of massive, flapping wings echoed above me. I whipped my head back to see a beast with an eagle's body in the front and a lion's body in the back.

Yup, I'd call that a classic gryphon, all right.

GRYPHON
LEVEL: 25,000
EXTRA BOSS: Suzuka Dungeon

AMANE RIN

LEVEL: 14,418   **SP:** 4,510

TITLES: Dungeon Traveler (10/10), Nameless Swordsman,
Endbringer (ERROR), Wiser Wise Man

HP: 112,500/112,500   **MP:** 23,150/31,680

ATTACK: 26,970   **DEFENSE:** 22,710   **SPEED:** 28,210

INTELLIGENCE: 22,370   **RESISTANCE:** 22,500   **LUCK:** 21,420

SKILLS: Dungeon Teleportation LV 21, Enhanced Strength LV MAX,
Herculean Strength LV MAX, Superhuman Strength LV MAX,
High-speed Movement LV MAX, Gale Wind LV MAX,
Revitalize LV 1, Purification Magic LV 1, Mana Boost LV MAX,
Mana Recovery LV 2, Enemy Detection LV 4, Evasion LV 4,
Status Condition Resistance LV 4, Appraisal, Item Box LV 6,
Conceal LV 1, Battle Barrier LV 1, Plunderer LV 1

The gryphon landed in front of me. Same as the Nameless Knight and the lightning beast, I had never read anything about this boss before. This would have to be a cautious fight where I slowly uncovered my enemy's abilities. And that level—25,000! Oof. This was easily the highest-level enemy I'd faced.

Yet I wasn't afraid. I'd survived enough clashes with overwhelming opponents to believe I could come out on top.

"Come to me, Nameless," I said, summoning the silver longsword to my right hand. I gripped it tightly and a flood of stat-boosting power washed over me like a sudden rainfall. Simultaneously, I activated Superhuman Strength and Gale Wind. My body thrummed with the electric promise of a summer thunderstorm.

"It's about time we get started, isn't it?"

I leapt like a discharged spark into the air, closing the distance between us at light speed. Propelled by kinetic energy, I swung Nameless—but something crucial became clear when it made contact.

"Is this what I think it is?!"

It was.

Invisible wind whipped around the gryphon's body in a protective barrier—just like the lightning beast and the salamander's elemental flame armor. A forceful gust buffeted me away from the gryphon. I neatly landed on the ground without damage, but now, I had to reconsider this whole fight.

What was my best option? Steal the wind armor, like I had against the salamander? The recommended level to beat the salamander was 10,000, and the MP it cost to steal its armor was over 20 percent. Stealing the gryphon's magic armor would cost double that, at a minimum. It was a hard sell.

The gryphon's shrill cry pierced the air—*and* my thoughts— as it descended in a counterattack. Those huge wings flapped fiercely, sending a violent squall my direction. The pressure was enough that it knocked me a few steps back.

I could overthink the gryphon later. Quelling that storm came first!

Should I dodge it? Not a bad idea, but I had a better one.

"Greed!" I shouted. The crimson sword appeared in my hand. I swung wide...and absorbed its attack, instead of its armor!

"Yes! Gotcha." A chartreuse gleam shone alongside the crimson light within the blade. I'd lost nearly a tenth of my MP, but I'd gained a new attack. This was a sweeter deal than the huge loss I'd incur stealing the armor.

Nameless, Greed, Time Zero, a fire bullet, and violent wind... how could I combine them to break the wind armor? The answer came quickly. As annoying as the armor was, it wasn't infallible. It couldn't hold a candle to the offensive electric shocks of the lightning beast's armor. The wind made things tricky by keeping me at bay, but that meant that the battle would be a cinch if I got close enough. I could do it if I relied on my skills and the boosted stats Nameless gave me.

My priority was to reach the gryphon's body. Forget clever strategizing; I decided to burst through the barrier with as much speed as I could muster.

"Here goes!" I shouted. I ran toward the gryphon. It was still in the air, but I paid that no mind.

Faster!

The gryphon changed its stance as if preparing to swoop down in an aerial strike. The only thing on my mind was gaining more speed.

Faster!!!

In less than a second, I felt myself reach full throttle. Before I really processed that, I had already leapt off the ground. The gryphon's lone defense was its barrier of wind, and at the rate I was going, I was sure to slam into it. But I wasn't out of tricks up my sleeve, so it wasn't going to happen.

Not to me.

"Time Zero."

I said the command and instantly teleported in front of the gryphon. As with all the other times I'd used this method, I retained my momentum; this was one of my key battle strategies at this point. Still, it wasn't enough to *maintain* my speed. I had to break through the gryphon's armor. I had to go faster, faster, *faster!*

I thrust Greed behind me and whispered, "Release."

The wind I'd stolen from the gryphon broke free from Greed and blasted away from me, propelling me forward. When the gryphon used its magic, its body clearly recoiled a little from the force of its own power. With my much lighter body using the same magic, the effect was amplified.

Faster than ever before, I flew at the gryphon with Nameless at the ready.

"Gooooooo!" I screamed.

With one slash, I shattered the armor and impaled my sword into the gryphon's face, eliciting a blood-curdling squeal from its gnashing beak. I drove the blade deeper into its body and then yanked up, slicing through muscle, skin, and feathers to leave a gaping hole in its body.

Its wings stilled in death, and the gryphon and I lost our inertia at the same time.

"Oops!" Forgot we were in midair.

I would have hit the ground in a heap if Time Zero hadn't buffered my landing. Nice one, Time Zero. The gryphon's dead-weight slammed down a second after I did.

The system rang in my head.

"You have defeated the extra boss."

"Gained XP: Level increased by 387!"

"Extra boss takedown reward: Level increased by 80!"

"Whew! I won."

Thanks to my double-level enemy, I gained a hefty dose of experience. I nodded with satisfaction and flicked Nameless a few times to shake off the rest of the blood. That gory work done, I examined Greed. It still swirled with crimson.

"Hey, and with magic to spare. Nice!"

Not a bad way to defeat Suzuka Dungeon.

AMANE RIN

LEVEL: 14,885   SP: 9,210

TITLES: Dungeon Traveler (10/10), Nameless Swordsman,
      Endbringer (ERROR), Wiser Wise Man

HP: 115,930/115,930   MP: 21,370/32,920

ATTACK: 26,970   DEFENSE: 22,710   SPEED: 28,210

INTELLIGENCE: 22,370   RESISTANCE: 22,500   LUCK: 21,420

SKILLS: Dungeon Teleportation LV 21, Enhanced Strength LV MAX,
      Herculean Strength LV MAX, Superhuman Strength LV MAX,
      High-speed Movement LV MAX, Gale Wind LV MAX,

Revitalize LV 1, Purification Magic LV 1, Mana Boost LV MAX, Mana Recovery LV 2, Enemy Detection LV 4, Evasion LV 4, Status Condition Resistance LV 4, Appraisal, Item Box LV 6, Conceal LV 1, Battle Barrier LV 1, Plunderer LV 1

With the gryphon felled, I could ponder my stats. I made a tuneless sound as I read through them.

"That fight with the Nameless Knight got me the Nameless Swordsman title, but this time I didn't get anything special," I said. "Guess it's fine. The gryphon wasn't too hard to beat."

Every little bit of experience counted, so I'd take that as its own reward.

I cut the magic stone from the gryphon's body and deposited the carcass into Item Box. I wasn't about to leave behind a level 25,000 monster. Based on its wind abilities, I assumed it would make good raw materials for wind-related equipment. Easy money, simple as that.

As for *how* I would sell it...

Selling an unknown monster wasn't as easy as spreading magic stones around to different shops so nobody noticed I had a weirdly high amount. As far as the public knew, this monster didn't even *exist*.

"Geez, this is bound to invite a lot of unwanted questions..."

A perfect opportunity to dump some responsibilities onto my new guild's plate!

"I'm not a full member, but I bet I could get someone to sell it for me. Ugh, but they might have questions of their own...better let it hibernate in Item Box for a while."

The gryphon carcass filled such a huge chunk of Item Box that I decided to spend 3,000 SP to boost Item Box from LV 6 to LV 8. Perfect.

Cleanup done, I waited until the dungeon's magic carried me to the Return Zone.

"What time is it now—*oh*." My watch revealed that I was inside the dungeon for less than an hour. I had the stamina for several more runs. "Well, fine. Time for round two. Dungeon Teleportation!"

My trademark skill delivered me to the boss room in no time. Naturally, the boss that spawned was a salamander. If I wanted an easy win, I could pull a repeat performance and steal its fire cloak with Greed, but that would hamstring my MP.

"Battle Barrier!"

I let the invisible barrier envelop my body and broke through the salamander's fire without a scratch. The skill was seriously handy, letting me come up with ad hoc battle strategies like this.

"*Dungeon Takedown Reward: Level increased by 50!*" the system informed me. This was my second dungeon takedown, meaning the extra boss didn't spawn.

"I'm gonna do the next one even faster!" I declared to no one in particular.

I looped the dungeon again at the same blistering pace.

"*Dungeon Takedown Reward: Level increased by 50!*"

"*Dungeon Takedown Reward: Level increased by 50!*"

"Dungeon Takedown Reward: Level increased by 50!"

My final dive count for the day at Suzuka? Nine runs through its depths.

As soon as I arrived home, I set about doling out the SP I'd accumulated.

"I've got 10,210 SP right now. I needed 10,000 to bring Battle Barrier to LV 2, didn't I? Think I'll go with that."

Battle Barrier had proved itself a versatile and powerful skill. If I buffed it for future battles, it ought to pay off in spades.

Take my battle with Yanagi: His skills were overpowered for his level, but his Attack stat was within the normal range. If his average strength could break through the barrier after a few firm hits, Battle Barrier wouldn't help me against high-level monsters. I had that on my mind as I opened my stats display to level up Battle Barrier, but something else caught my eye first.

> Dungeon Teleportation LV 21 → LV 22 (SP NEEDED: 10,000)
> Battle Barrier LV 1 → LV 2 (SP NEEDED: 10,000)

"Hold up. Boosting Dungeon Teleportation costs the *same* amount as last time?"

LV 21 cost 10,000 SP, hadn't it? I thought for sure the next level up would cost at least 15,000 or 20,000 SP. Huh...unexpected.

"I'll be grinding Suzuka for a while longer, so I might as well pick Dungeon Teleportation. Nice as it'd be to upgrade Battle Barrier, this is too tempting."

This could lead to another dramatic evolution! Hopeful, I invested the SP.

"Dungeon Teleportation has increased to LV 22."

"Teleportation distance has changed."

"Maximum 400 meters → Maximum 600 meters."

"Jeez...frickin' waste of SP." Talk about a real letdown.

What good did an extra two hundred meters do me? I'd gotten used to my skill growth falling short of my expectations, so I wasn't *that* bummed about it...but it wasn't what I expected all the same. Just in case, I checked how much SP it would take to reach LV 23. Another 10,000 points.

"Does that mean the skill's done transforming? Should I prioritize Battle Barrier in the meantime?"

I didn't have the answer, so I would decide somewhere down the line. With my head full of questions, I ate the dinner Hana made for us and went to bed.

I spent the next day grinding Suzuka. Needless to say, I used Dungeon Teleportation to get inside.

Every time I said, "Dungeon Teleportation," a floating sensation washed over my body. By now, it was as familiar as walking to me. Teleport, float, descend, land. I repeated those four steps down to the lowest level where the boss room awaited.

"Haaa!" I shouted, brandishing Greed against the salamander. I activated Battle Barrier. One-hit KOs weren't possible even at this stage, but multiple attacks at the speed of sound helped me win unscathed.

The system rang out.

"You have defeated the dungeon boss."

"Dungeon Takedown Reward: Level increased by 50!"

I was sick of hearing that. Couldn't a guy get some new background music, like a jaunty tune in a video game? I resignedly stuffed the salamander's body—and the Mana Amplification Stone I received as the takedown reward—into Item Box.

"Smooth sailing so far," I said.

The return spell activated and returned me to the surface, where I challenged Suzuka anew. Lather, rinse, repeat. Over and over.

"Dungeon Takedown Reward: Level increased by 50!"

"Dungeon Takedown Reward: Level increased by 50!"

"Dungeon Takedown Reward: Level increased by 50!"

"Dungeon Takedown Reward..."

No extra bosses spawned, yesterday's gryphon or otherwise, so I beat the dungeon over thirty times without breaking a sweat.

I used my SP spoils to boost Battle Barrier to LV 2 that night and put it to the test the next day. I took a hit from the salamander's fire on purpose. Compared to when the skill was at LV 1, its defensive capacity was nearly doubled. Great, then it was worth the SP investment—which was more than I could say for Dungeon Teleportation.

"This skill's gonna be so useful against strong enemies as it levels up. Glad to have it," I said with relish. Maybe Dungeon Teleportation would hear me and step up its game.

I looped the dungeon yet again, and in no time, the system rang out.

"*You have reached this dungeon's maximum number of allotted victories.*"

"*Bonus Reward: Level increased by 120!*"

"*You will no longer receive rewards for defeating this dungeon.*"

I'd ground my way through fifty runs before I received the notification.

"Cool. Take that, Suzuka!"

Riding high on adrenaline, I opened my stats display to review the growth recorded there.

AMANE RIN

LEVEL: 17,455   SP: 6,910

TITLES: Dungeon Traveler (10/10), Nameless Swordsman,
Endbringer (ERROR), Wiser Wise Man

HP: 136,450/136,450   MP: 21,920/38,100

ATTACK: 32,570   DEFENSE: 27,420   SPEED: 34,140

INTELLIGENCE: 27,080   RESISTANCE: 27,210   LUCK: 26,130

SKILLS: Dungeon Teleportation LV 22, Enhanced Strength LV MAX,
Herculean Strength LV MAX, Superhuman Strength LV MAX,

High-speed Movement LV MAX, Gale Wind LV MAX,
Revitalize LV 1, Purification Magic LV 1, Mana Boost LV MAX,
Mana Recovery LV 2, Enemy Detection LV 4, Evasion LV 4,
Status Condition Resistance LV 4, Appraisal, Item Box LV 8,
Conceal LV 1, Battle Barrier LV 2, Plunderer LV 1

Suzuka was maxed out, but the day was still young. Problem was, I'd beaten every B-rank dungeon within commutable distance. Since I didn't have enough time to reach one of the faraway ones, I ultimately called it a day. On my walk to the train station, I considered what I would need to prep if I traveled out-of-town to a dungeon.

"Man, d'you see that girl just now? She was gorgeous!" a nearby student said.

"I know, right?"

Their conversation snagged my interest. Not to say I was *that* interested in the girl's appearance, but who wouldn't be curious? I looked ahead and saw an arcade amidst a line of storefronts. A glamorous girl stood in front of a crane game machine, exactly as they said. Her silver hair drew stares as it glinted in the afternoon sun.

Is that who I think it is?

Who else could it be than Claire, Yoizuki Guild member, S-rank adventurer, twelfth in Japan, in that exact order. Should I say hello or slide on past her? I might make it weird...

Before I could decide, Claire decisively lifted her arm and pushed a 100-yen coin into the game.

Her expression turned serious, her deep blue eyes narrowing. She seemed to be after a specific prize. I followed her gaze to a wolf plushie with a giant head. It had a black eyepatch over its right eye and a scar over its left eye. Could it see at all?

Wait, I recognized that character... It was Wolfun! Wolfun was from a children's TV show that aired on Sunday mornings called Magical Dungeon Girls—otherwise known as Magidun, for short.

Magidun was a friendship-heavy action story about girls who awaken to a unique skill called "Magical Girl" and save people from monsters. A dungeon collapses in the first episode (not as much of a disaster as it would be in real life) and introduces Wolfun, the show's mascot. He's an unusual life-form that allies with any human with the will to tame him. He speaks in a crude, borderline inappropriate way and has the eyepatch and scar to give him a tough appearance.

Kids didn't connect to him at all because of his rough way of acting and speaking. Funnily enough, that was precisely what earned Wolfun an adult fan base. They thought his gruff ways were endearing.

Blame Hana for why I knew all of this. I used to watch it every Sunday morning with her. Mind you, I only watched it as a way to spend time with her, but the story was more engaging than I expected.

Oh yeah, Rei was a Magidun fan too. She and Hana texted

each other about it. I admit, I could get so caught up in fan theories myself that we talked about the show through dinner and past midnight.

Okay, hold on, not the time to fall into the Magidun theory pit: back to the topic at hand. Claire was in front of me, vying for her prize.

Her eyes flashed as she pressed the button. The crane descended toward Wolfun and wrapped around his body so, so tantalizingly. Claire stared intensely as it lifted his chunky form up in the air—and promptly dropped him.

"Aww," she said.

The crane's arm was rigged to be too weak to grip him properly, but that didn't deter her. She tried again and again *and* again. Maybe she hadn't played many crane games. After ten similar losses, she clearly didn't know how to finesse it.

I shouldn't just stand and watch. But should I help her?

What if she got embarrassed, knowing that some guy she barely knew was watching her take a crane game so seriously? I didn't want to put her in that position. An S-rank adventurer definitely had money to burn on silly games. She could buy the whole arcade and not break the bank.

Yeah, I was better off ignoring this!

"Amane-san?" she said.

"Uhhh."

Whoops. Famous last words. She noticed me, and now things were awkward. Panic overtook her face.

"H-h-how long have you been there?" she asked.

Even I could tell she was asking whether I'd seen her lose so many times. I couldn't admit I'd watched her from the start. *Dang it.* Emergency subject change!

"Oh hey, this is just trivia, but did you know that most prizes at this arcade cost less than 800 yen?"

"Why are you bringing that up?"

"Oh, you practically spent double that...so, uh... y'know."

She glared at me. Oh god, I freaked out and seriously messed up! I couldn't pretend I only saw her try once anymore. I hadn't expected her to *interrogate* me. I was a little afraid she'd turn me into a smear on the sidewalk. Claire was an S-rank adventurer, after all.

Instead, she released a small sigh and her cheeks tinged a soft rose-gold pink.

"It's my fault for letting my guard down, so I won't reprimand you," she said, "but I hope you'll alert me to your presence sooner next time."

"I'll do that, for sure, no problem," I agreed, practically nodding my head off.

It *was* creepy of me to rubberneck while she failed at the crane game. I thought of a way to apologize, at least.

"Let me step in," I said.

"Huh?"

She was confused, but she stepped aside and let me face the machine. I slipped a coin in and the crane whirred to life.

In the past, when I was watching over Hana, she'd often beg me to catch her a stuffed animal or some other crane prize. After playing a bunch of these games for her, I wasn't too shabby at them. The trick wasn't to catch the stuffed animal with the crane itself. It would take a few tries, but the best method was to lift and rework its position until it fell into the hole. That said, there was an even better way to snag this one.

I finagled the forward and back buttons until I had the arms dangling where I wanted them. As they descended toward the item next to Wolfun, Claire said, "Won't it miss Wolfun from that angle?"

"Trust the process!"

Like I expected, the arm caught Wolfun's tag and hoisted him up.

"Using such an impressive technique...!" she said, clearly shocked.

The machine brought Wolfun to the hole and safely dropped it. I withdrew the stuffed animal from the flap.

"I'm surprised," she said, her voice carrying a new respect. "I had no idea you were a crane game expert."

"Yeah, my sister used to badger me to play them a lot. I'm more surprised that *you* like Wolfun so much."

"You know where Wolfun's from?!"

She leaned in close as she asked. With her unusual hair swaying so close, the sweet scent of her shampoo wafted over me. I caught myself leaning backward without meaning to, but I regained my composure enough to reply.

"Sure, I do. I watch Magidun every week," I said. "Anyway, you're sort of close to me..."

"Ah, sorry!"

Her face reddened and she hastily stepped back. She must have closed the distance between us without realizing. In the absence of her presence, I didn't know whether to be relieved or disappointed. Both emotions in my chest snapped at each other like wolves while she apologized.

"My sincerest apologies, Amane-san," she said. "I don't have many people I can talk to about Wolfun. I forgot my manners."

"Don't worry about it. Here you go."

I proffered the Wolfun plush to her like a bouquet, but she only stared at it in question. I guessed she didn't understand the gesture, so I clarified.

"For you," I said.

"For...me?"

"Yeah."

"But you won it. I can't take him from another Wolfun fan. That would be blasphemous!"

At some point, I transformed into a Wolfun fan in her eyes, but I was not about to give up. I gestured insistently with it.

"Please, don't worry about that. I wanted to give it to you from the start. You'd be helping me if you took it."

"...If you insist."

Her expression was surprisingly timid, but she took it with both hands.

What was going through her head? She stared at the stuffed animal in silence for a few seconds, then hugged it like it was precious. She turned her soft smile toward me.

"Thank you, Amane-san. I'm really, really happy."

That smile quickened my pulse. Was my own face heating up? Suddenly, a ringtone cut in and distracted us—her phone, not mine.

"My father is calling," Claire said. "Please wait a minute?"

"Sure."

She stuck Wolfun under her left arm and answered the phone. "Hello?"

"Claire? Thank goodness you answered. I need your input on something. Is now a good time?"

"...Yes, no problem," she answered, glancing at me as she stepped away.

The conversation sounded important, so she wanted her privacy. I suddenly felt quite alone, but it would be rude to wander off, so I stuck around until she finished her call. About two minutes passed before she hung up and walked back.

Or not. She still had her phone to her ear. What was up? Her conversation with the guild master leaked out of the phone's speaker, loud enough for me to hear.

"Okay, Claire," he said. "If you say so, I'll give Amane a call."

"No need," she replied. "Amane-san is with me, so I'll check with him. I'll call you back once I have an answer."

"Huh?! *Hold on*. What business does he have with my adorable daught—"

The phone beeped as she hung up and cut him off. I forced a smile. With only the tail end of that conversation, I wasn't sure how to react.

"Sounds like he cares about you a lot," I tried.

She pouted indignantly. Swing and a miss. "Too much, in my opinion!"

If nothing else, it seemed like they were close?

"So, what did he want?" I asked. "I heard my name."

"Yes, that's the issue at hand. Ignore everything else my father said."

Oof, brutal, Claire. I could picture her father crying if he heard that.

She continued. "Amane-san, since you're a provisionary member of Yoizuki, you agreed to dive with a high-rank guild member to evaluate our usefulness to you. Do you remember the conversation?"

"Yeah, of course." I remembered well. She must be asking because...

"Does this mean I finally have my invitation?" I asked.

"Yes, but there are two complications."

"Complications?"

"Affirmative. First, the dive date is tomorrow, which I know is rather sudden. Are you currently impacted by the Span?"

After a short pause, I shook my head. "No, I'm good on that front."

A total lie, since I was on my way home from beating a dungeon *right then*. I didn't need to worry about it, I hoped. Dungeon Teleportation's boosted skill level would let me enter any dungeon I wanted. As long as I was careful about how I went past the Gate, no one would find out.

Tomorrow was still *very* sudden, though. Thanks to the Span, when people planned dives together, they usually gave over one week's notice. I doubted a guild master would forget something like that, so there must be a different reason for such late notice.

"The second complication is more serious," Claire said. "The dungeon in question will be a new dungeon—one that spawned this morning."

I gulped without thinking. A brand-new dungeon? No one in the world knew anything about it, from monster encounters to traps. The danger level was incomparable to other dungeons.

In most cases, a dungeon's first challengers would be high-rank adventurers (especially guild members) that were drafted to work with the Dungeon Association to create takedown records. Yoizuki must've been assigned the task this time around.

Obtaining information about a new dungeon was urgent business. That explained the suddenness of this invitation. The issue was whether or not I should accept it. I didn't have enough information to jump into danger yet.

"Can I ask a few questions?"

"Certainly. I'll answer what I can."

Claire was the one who spoke to the guild master, so she knew much more than me about the situation. I wanted that info.

She answered my questions, but maybe that didn't matter.

Deep down, my mind was made up. To see the extent of a Yoizuki Guild member's power, I needed a place like a new dungeon—a fresh fighting ground where no one knew what could happen. My curiosity was piqued beyond my ability to suppress it.

There were plenty of reasons to want to go. One run around that dungeon would surely boost my level at a frightening speed, but that wasn't the only draw. I knew there was way more to strength than leveling up.

The Nameless Knight, orc general, lightning beast, Yanagi—all of those stronger enemies put my abilities to the test and pushed me to dig deeper. I was at my best under pressure. If powerful, unforeseen enemies awaited me in that dungeon, how could I not take them on?

My drive to grow was relentless. That was why I'd already made my decision.

"That's the extent of the answers I can give you," Claire said, finishing. "If you want more information, you'll need to consult my father directly."

"That's okay. You told me enough," I said. "I want to join the team dive."

THE WORLD'S FASTEST
LEVEL UP

CHAPTER 3

TEAM DIVE

THE VERY NEXT DAY, I traveled to a suburb just outside the city for the team dive. That was where the new dungeon happened to form.

I looked left and right, taking in the neighborhood. Homes spread out in every direction, but not a single civilian showed themselves near the dungeon. I wouldn't have expected otherwise. No one was permitted within range of a new, and therefore potentially dangerous, dungeon without explicit permission. The same thing occurred when the Remote Magic Tower appeared.

The only humans around were the eight figures in front of the dungeon entrance. As I drew closer, I noticed they were decked out in top-notch dive gear. Expensive armor, elaborate robes, things like that.

That's an A-rank party for you. Those B-rank adventurers I saw didn't hold a candle to their vibe.

I thought back to the rundown Claire gave me yesterday. Prior to exploring a new dungeon for the first time, the dungeon's difficulty level had to be investigated. Tossing a special item through the Gate provided a measurement on the dungeon's internal mana levels, which made it possible to determine whether the dungeon was C-rank or below, or whether it was B-rank or above. In the case of C-rank or below, any party with experience in B-rank dungeons could take on the first task of exploration, so long as they were careful. If the dungeon was B-rank or above, an A-rank party—rare even for Japan—would take it over.

In the case of this new dungeon, the mana measurement suggested a minimum level requirement of 10,000 to enter. Because of that, Claire said Yoizuki would send in their only A-rank party.

Since Claire was an obvious outlier as an S-rank, she didn't come today. To be honest, she was the one I wanted to dive with most. Too bad.

Regardless, the people standing before me were overwhelmingly strong, the top 1 percent of adventurers. I was part of the other 99 percent. I needed to buck up and get on their level.

Once I reached the group, I noticed a familiar face. If I was right, his name was Yagami-san. He was the man who drove me and Claire to Yoizuki. According to Claire, he was the party's leader.

So, not just a driver after all. Whatever he was, it was only polite to greet him first.

"I'm Amane Rin," I said. "Good to see you today."

"Tsk. You really came?" he replied.

Jeez, rude much. What was *his* problem?

He'd reacted similarly when we first met, hadn't he? I didn't understand why he hated me so much. At least the other party members looked at me with interest instead of annoyance. The guild master must've told them about me. Even if they weren't hostile, my guess was they didn't think a young guy like me had any business diving a dungeon of this rank. Couldn't blame them; in their position, I would've felt the same way. Unfortunately, I needed them to tolerate me for a while.

Yagami-san eyed me with a quick, irritated glance.

"Just so you know, you're only here because our guild master ordered it. Stay back and *don't fight anything*. That's the one condition, and if you break that, we'll leave you behind."

"I understand," I said with a nod. That didn't sound different from the conditions I heard yesterday, so I wasn't complaining. I didn't want to be the one who broke their party formations either. My goal was understanding just how powerful they really were. Causing problems wouldn't do me any favors.

Once everyone finished their final gear checks, we entered the Return Zone. With our leader Yagami-san at the helm, we entered the Gate one by one.

Last in line to go through, I exhaled.

Okay...I'm in this for the long haul.

I had no idea where any of the stairs were inside—*no one* did—so I couldn't breeze through the levels. Each step of progress would be careful, constantly wary of monsters and traps. The time it took to beat this dungeon the first time would be multiplied exponentially compared to an already-mapped dungeon. In the worst case, a new B-rank dungeon could take a week to conquer.

Good thing I warned Hana ahead of time that I wouldn't make it home. Just like when I left for the Remote Magic Tower, she grinned and asked me if I was leaving for a sleepover with a *girlfriend*. I didn't know why, but hearing that question shot ice up my spine. Her smile only made it scarier.

Seriously, what the heck was that all about?

No clue, but while I was thinking, my turn to cross the Gate came. Technically, I was in the middle of a Span, so I couldn't pass through. I used my skill instead.

"Dungeon Teleportation."

I landed inside, finding myself alongside the eight people who entered before me. But something felt...off. The sensation was difficult to explain, almost as if the dungeon itself existed with a different air than other dungeons.

Suddenly, Yagami-san whirled on me and said, "Hey, you. Go back outside the Gate and come back in."

"Huh?"

"I'm checking something. Hurry it up."

At first, I didn't understand what he was getting at, but then the words *checking something* made sense.

In rare cases, once an adventurer crossed the Gate, they couldn't leave until they defeated the boss. Also, if they left through the Gate, they couldn't try the dungeon again regardless of whether the Span was in effect. First-challenger teams were duty-bound to check that kind of thing.

If this dungeon was subject to the latter case, it made sense for me to be the one stuck outside. In an elite group like this, I was the least useful in battle. As much as I understood where he was coming from, I couldn't do it. Even worse, I couldn't explain why to Yagami-san. I *had* to use Dungeon Teleportation to pass through this Gate. I wouldn't give an accurate test result. Combative as it would come across, I had to refuse.

"I can't do that," I said.

"Excuse me?" His stare sharpened. "Did you get a big head or something? You think you can contribute to beating this dungeon more than the rest of us?"

"No, that's not what I meant..."

"Then tell me what you *did* mean. If you don't, I'll assume you think you can make it to the last floor on your own. A guy who's that deluded will put the rest of this party in danger."

"Urk!"

Dang it, why was he talking sense? He only made me feel worse about refusing. I shut my mouth. I had to keep my secret, but Yagami-san's glare only grew narrower. Refusing to speak *really* provoked him. I felt bad for seeming insubordinate, but what could I do?

To my gratitude, one of the others stepped forward—a pretty, delicate woman dressed in a robe. "Now, now, take it easy, Yagami-san. I'll do it."

"Don't be ridiculous, Shinonome. We can't lose our only healer." He sighed. "Fine. Matsumoto, you go."

"I feel like you just called me the most useless!" a man in sorcerer garb who must have been Matsumoto complained. "Yagami-san, I'll do it for you."

He exited the Gate, then returned a second later.

"No issue with reentry," he said.

"Okay. Let's proceed," Yagami-san said. He glared at me one final time, then turned and followed the two tanks at the helm. At the rear of the group was me and the woman who bailed me out. I ducked my head to her in a mixture of apology and thanks.

"Sorry about that. You really saved me," I said.

"Ha ha ha! Don't worry about it. The way Yagami-san phrased it, it was like he said 'Amane-kun, you're a big liability!' I totally get why you'd push back."

"Mmm..."

Seemed I'd tarred myself with the label of prideful kid with that stunt, but I let it go. The misunderstanding was a good cover story.

Shinonome-san smiled warmly. "I'm Shinonome Kaori, by the way. You can call me Shinonome-san, Kaori-chan, Oneesan—whatever you want."

"Nice to meet you, Shinonome-san. I'm—"

Hold on. I was about to introduce myself when I remembered she'd called me Amane-kun. I hadn't said my name since joining the group. Had she really remembered it?

Shinonome smiled again. "Your name is Amane Rin-kun, right? Of course, I know *you*."

"I guess you would know the name of the new guy joining your party."

"That's part of it, but I knew about you before this. You've piqued my interest, Amane-kun."

"What?" I blinked at her.

"Your name comes up when I talk to Yui-chan and Rei-chan."

Their names explained a lot. "Are you close with the two of them?" I asked.

"Oh yes. As a healer, I'm something of a mentor to Yui-chan. I've been teaching her since she joined. And I talk to Rei-chan here and there."

"Are they doing well in Yoizuki?"

"Of course! Yui-chan is incredible. Her talent as a healer keeps growing, and I don't think it's a stretch to say she'll be a real battle asset for the guild in the near future. As for Rei-chan..." Her expression became somewhat reserved. "She has a unique skill, so she can't be measured on the usual scale. What I *do* know is that her skill is quite..."

She looked up in surprise, as if she'd tripped on something invisible. "Actually, I'll leave it at that. You two are close, so you should talk to her yourself."

"Sure, I mean, I'll do that."

I was curious what she wouldn't say, but it would be bad to hear it from Shinonome. Next time I met up with Rei, I'd ask her about it, just the two of us.

She deftly changed the subject to the party. "If you'd like to know what we're like, I'll give you a run-down of the basics. Our party has eight members, and most of us are over level 20,000. Yagami-san is the only one over level 25,000."

"Makes sense." I knew Yagami-san was the leader, so I figured he would be the highest level. "This is the top party in Yoizuki, right?"

"As a party, yes. Claire-chan is stronger than all of us on her own."

I considered that. Claire was an S-rank. Anyone S-rank had to be over level 100,000. Yeah. Compared to everyone here, there *was* no comparison.

"How did she..." I trailed off. *How* Claire obtained that kind of power nagged at me. As a member of the same guild, maybe Shinonome-san knew the answer. On second thought, it was wrong to try to dig up her secrets this way. I changed my question.

"What's Claire's position in the guild?" I asked.

"Position?"

"Not her job, per se. I guess I mean how other guild members view her. Does her power put distance between her and her guildmates?"

Shinonome-san chuckled. "That's a funny question, Amane-kun, but mm... Claire-chan is closed off from everyone. As impressive as her power is, she doesn't show off, and she's polite to a fault, but there's something else." She paused. "Maybe that power is exactly what makes her so polite. I get the feeling she's built an invisible barrier between herself and others."

"A barrier?"

"Mm-hm. Like she's avoiding growing closer to people than necessary."

I thought back to my past encounters with Claire. The first day I met her, she was mellow yet pointed in the way she spoke to me, beautiful and straight-up *cool* when she killed the cyclops in one strike. Then there was the time she made me eat a snack, and the way she'd hugged the Wolfun stuffed animal yesterday.

Wait. What was Shinonome-san talking about? None of that seemed avoidant to *me*. I furrowed my brow a little.

"That's just the impression I get," she said. "If you're asking, does that mean she's caught your eye?"

"N-not in *that* way..."

"Tee hee. Sorry, kiddo, but you can't fool this Oneesan's keen eyes one bit. Lots of people have their eye on Claire-chan, so you're in for a tough fight. But I'm rooting for you!"

This conversation went places I did not expect! Chills of trepidation, almost as cold as the ones from Hana's ominous grin, ran through me.

"*Ahem*," Yagami-san cut in. "Shinonome, monsters could spawn any second now. Leave the chit-chat and gossip for later."

"Hmph. Just when it was getting good..." she pouted. "Yes, sir!"

She pouted, but the questions stopped. *Whew.* Who would expect Yagami-san with the save? I was genuinely grateful, even though we didn't encounter a monster for another five minutes.

It happened as we were traveling the first floor. All of a sudden, the sound of inhuman footsteps reached us. Yagami-san reacted quickly.

"Take positions!" he ordered.

They obeyed his instruction and stepped into formation. Beside them, I drew a weapon from my Item Box.

SPEED SWORD

A short sword made with a Blacksmith skill.

RECOMMENDED EQUIP LEVEL: 7,000

ATTACK +6,000

SPEED +3,500

Speed Sword was the best choice here, not Nameless or Greed. Both were unknown weapons, so I didn't want to show them to anyone else yet.

Five monsters stood before us. They were bipedal monsters with tough, pointed, almost hedgehog-like fur:

WEREWOLF

LEVEL: 8,000

A bipedal beast with fur tough enough to repel a blade. Swift and agile, it wields sharp claws and fangs to land powerful attacks.

The dang things stood about as tall as human adults, and their level demonstrated exactly how tough their bodies were.

But for an A-rank party, they were hardly a challenge.

"Fireline!" Yagami-san shouted.

The tanks drew the werewolves' attention and showered them in attacks, which created openings that Yagami-san used to land fire spells to finish them off. The five werewolves went down in less than a minute.

His work done, Yagami-san grunted in satisfaction.

They definitely didn't need my help. Watching their combo

attack was reassuring, and the total opposite of the self-indulgent showoffery of Kazami and the rest of the Kings of Unique.

"We didn't contribute at all," Shinonome-san said.

"Not even a bit," I commiserated.

Yagami-san nodded, thought it was more to himself than to us. "Against monsters of this level, we should fight with MP preservation in mind. Remember that as you battle."

"Roger!" the party said in unison.

Progress was smooth as well-oiled machinery after that. We used Enemy Detection to find the stairs to the next floor and defeated the monsters in our way, leaving signs and signals in the ground along the way to track our path. We had to move forward through trial and error, which meant the length of the journey stretched like warm New Year's mochi, much more than the journey through a familiar dungeon would. For nine floors, we managed to make it through without facing any real danger.

After a short break, we walked down the stairs to the tenth floor.

Doubt crept up to me and practically tapped me on the shoulder.

What's this weird sensation...?

That *off* feeling niggling at me since I stepped foot inside the dungeon was growing stronger the deeper we went. I'd brought it up, but no one else felt it, so we were pressing on like it was nothing. Was it really all in my head?

I soon found out that my concern came from something very, very real. I absolutely should have trusted my gut.

◆⌃◆

On floor thirty, a giant goblin king over two meters tall and eight orc general minions appeared in front of us. While the tanks held off the goblin king, the rest of the team wiped out the minions, then focused on the king. Just when the goblin king made itself vulnerable, Yagami-san shouted an order.

"Now! *Whale* on it!"

The knight in front crashed forward like a tsunami and slashed his longsword at the goblin king's torso. The goblin king bellowed in rage, only to succumb and collapse a few moments later.

Thus far, that level 14,000 monster was the strongest enemy they'd faced, but it was still easy for such a capable party to handle.

"At this rate, I really will be stuck observing," I grumbled at the rear. Man, I wanted to fight! But they were too awesome for any danger to come my way. It was a good thing that they were so strong, but what was this feeling? *Dreary* might be the word for it.

Just when I was about to breathe the feeling out, I shivered like someone had dumped a bucket of cold water on me.

"What was that?!"

I panicked and glanced around me, unable to ignore such a chill. Something terrible was about to happen—and I wasn't basing this on nothing! I'd experienced a fear like this before at the Remote Magic Tower, a dungeon where *everything* about it was unlike the usual dungeons. Heck, I still thought a few of its challenges were *designed* to kill me.

Strength, Intelligence, Mana, Stamina. Those quests challenged every ability I had as an adventurer, leaving no room for me to relax for a measly second. The tower taught me to tap into a *much* stronger instinct for impending danger, and that instinct was telling me to put my guard up.

But...with the goblin king down, what was there to be wary about? I kept looking around suspiciously like a teenager in a horror movie. Danger could be anywhere.

"Whew. Based on the difficulty of that monster, I'd say there are probably sixty or seventy floors total," Shinonome-san said brightly. She took a deep breath, relaxed after the surety of killing a monster. "This is where it gets real. We'd better keep it up!"

For a second, when my eyes fell on the goblin king's heap of a body, I thought I saw its finger twitch. I was about to brush it off when the whole body lurched upright.

"Shinonome, get back!" Yagami-san shouted.

"What?" she said.

Only me and Yagami-san realized what was happening. Shinonome-san's eyes widened in bewilderment at the reanimated goblin king, which raised its longsword over its head. She screamed.

"Dammit!" Yagami-san swore.

We were both almost ten meters away from her, out of range to help. Shinonome-san tried to jump back, and Yagami-san launched a spell in the monster's direction, but he wouldn't make it in time.

There was only one way to save her.

"Time Zero," I said without hesitation. In the next moment, the goblin king's head went flying, and the rest of its body fell backward with a thud. Me and my Speed Sword landed where the monster had been standing.

"Huh?" Shinonome-san yelped in surprise when she saw me. "What just—?!"

She tried to back away quickly but ended up nearly falling over, so I caught her.

"Whoa there," I said.

Our faces were *very* close, and her chest was pressed firmly up against mine. Somehow, I managed to push *that* detail away.

"Are you okay?" I asked.

She nodded swiftly, her face bright red. She seemed fine, so that was a relief. Once she found her feet, I let her go and looked at the others.

As I expected, none of them missed what I'd done.

Well, I had to say *something*. How would I explain this away?

Yagami-san spoke first, his voice tense as he made no move to hide his unrest. "What did you just...do?" he asked.

Out of all of them, he *definitely* saw the moment I teleported back into existence. He had questions, of course.

"I specialize in Speed," I said, facing him. "I use a skill that erases my presence when monsters spawn. It only looks like I disappear."

It was a poor excuse. He hadn't mentioned the part where I appeared out of nowhere, so maybe I'd just drawn *more* suspicion onto myself. I really screwed this up.

"You expect me to buy that explanation?" Yagami-san said. He shook his head as if to force himself to accept my words. "No, guild master says it's not my business."

He turned so I couldn't see his face. Was he *embarrassed* for some reason?

"Whatever you used, you saved a member of this party so... thank you."

"Um, you're welcome?" I said, shocked by his sudden attitude shift.

He focused his gaze on the goblin king. "We need to investigate how this thing could move after we killed it. C'mon, Amane."

Wow. He actually used my name. He was starting to accept me.

"Yes, sir!" I said with a smile.

The goblin king's reanimation was not a one-time occurrence. A small fraction of the monsters we encountered after that also returned to life. Determined to discover the cause, we investigated each corpse until we formed a hypothesis.

"It really seems to be true," Yagami-san marveled. "They can come back to life if a magic stone remains inside them."

"*And* the higher the monster's level, the more likely it is to happen," Shinonome added. "The goblin generals we defeated earlier didn't resurrect themselves even with their magic stones intact."

"Yes, level appears to be a factor too. This will be a real headache," Yagami-san said. "To ensure a kill, we either destroy the magic stone before they go down or behead them like Amane did. We have to be more careful as we fight and make sure the stones are destroyed even though it's akin to burning money."

He considered the facts for a few seconds, then came to a conclusion. "If we're right and a monster must be high level to come back to life, then it'll happen more often the deeper we go. I say we rest for a few hours on a safer upper floor and continue downward later. Everyone okay with that?"

"Yes, sir!" we replied with a round of nodding.

I agreed with Yagami-san's prudent decision. Defeating monsters was easy for this party, but worrying about which monsters would respawn took a psychological toll. To rest and regroup was the best path forward.

Although, if I was *alone*, I would've kept going.

We took to formation again and were trekking back to a safe floor when the dungeon began to tremble.

"What's going on?!" said one of the party members. Another member screamed.

Alarm at the sudden change swept through the party members—and I wasn't above it. What was this? The first possibility that jumped to mind was a dungeon collapse, but something about that wasn't right. From the way the dungeon vibrated to the clattering sounds that echoed inside, if I had to guess, I'd say it was a—

"Hey, look, over there!" shouted one of the party members. He pointed in the direction of the clamor. "That *better* not be what I think it is!"

Like a family of meerkats, we turned our heads in unison in the direction of his pointing finger—and got a vicious shock.

A stampede of over fifty monsters barreled toward us from the way we'd walked from. They were charging toward us, but their eyes were unfocused, like we didn't even register to them.

I bit my lip in horror, then shouted the name of this phenomenon.

"Monster swarm!"

Like the name suggested, a monster swarm was a phenomenon where a large number of monsters appeared at the same time and swarmed the dungeon. Each monster swarm had a different trigger, from stepping in a monster spawn point to pure coincidence. The trigger this time was the latter, I suspected.

Monster swarms occurred regardless of rank or dungeon, but they were never much of an issue for me. Worst-case scenario, I used Dungeon Teleportation to bail myself out. Unfortunately, for normal adventurers, these encounters were life-threatening.

"Tanks in front!" Yagami-san ordered.

"Yes, sir!"

The two tanks formed a defense to stop the monsters. The path was narrow, so they succeeded in slowing the horde, but that left the others without much space to launch attacks. The monsters would break our defense in a matter of time. The group desperately considered ways to fight back.

"Leader, monsters are coming from over here too!" Shinonome-san shouted.

"A different direction?!" Yagami-san yelled.

What Shinonome-san said was true. As if their plan were to utterly drown us, another large group of monsters charged us from the opposite direction.

Normal monster swarms didn't operate like this. Something was definitely wrong. I grit my teeth in frustration. Everyone was frozen in dismay and confusion, but Yagami-san rallied us with a firm order.

"Retreat! This won't end well!" he shouted. "I'll use ranged magic on them while we find an open area! Move it!"

Those of us in the rear were now the frontline as we fled through the only tunnel available. Yagami-san and the others followed behind me and Shinonome-san.

"There's another horde up ahead!" warned one of them.

"Not down this path! Go!"

As we encountered more forks in the road, most of them had an army of monsters lying in wait. Each time, we found an empty tunnel and pushed onward. Along the way, that *off* feeling buzzed in the pit of my stomach again. There were so many monster swarms that the empty tunnels felt like a path sketched by some unseen hand.

"Something's wrong," I muttered. "This is getting suspicious..."

I didn't know why *this many* monsters had spawned, but if the dungeon wanted to kill us outright, wouldn't it flood *all* of the tunnels? Yet, somehow, we kept finding escape routes laid out as tantalizing as cheese for a mouse.

We were being *baited*. That was the only conclusion I could reach. As much as I didn't like what was happening, we couldn't stop. Not even revealing my hidden powers would bail us out of this situation. The best option was to obey Yagami-san and follow his wealth of battle experience.

My head knew that, but my heart wouldn't stop racing. Our retreating feet pounded the rocky floor of the dungeon until we reached our final destination.

"Look, there's a big room over there!" Shinonome-san said, delighted. "That should give us room to fight back!"

No one hesitated. We slipped through the passage that led to the open space, but when we stepped inside, a shiver coursed through my body.

"What was that?" I said, whirling around. The prickling I felt was completely new.

Yagami-san showered the monsters that pursued us with magic and miraculously made it into the room. The room that I realized was flanked by two open doors.

"Get outside!!" I screamed.

Yagami-san heard me and widened his eyes. "What're you talking about, Amane? A *legion* of monsters is out there. We have to defeat them or we won't—"

He never finished his sentence. The deafening sound of the doors slamming shut drowned him out.

"What was that? The doors shut behind us?"

"Did we make it past the swarm?"

The others were confused by the sight, but the closed doors calmed them despite their surprise. My heart didn't stop racing, so I couldn't share in their relief. If my hunch was right...

"E-everyone, turn around," Yagami-san said, voice trembling. His stare trailed *upward*. I took a deep breath, turned slowly, then saw *it*.

I knew this was coming.

A monster reminiscent of the orc general pulled itself out of the wall, where it towered at least five meters above us. Two giant fangs hung from its mouth, and its stony body was painted a muddy red. Something about it emitted an odd, unnatural air. Its thick hands grasped a greatsword that was almost half its body length.

Fear quickly engulfed everyone there.

"No way. We're not even on the last floor. Why is something so strong *here*?"

"Was this a trick?!"

I quietly used Appraisal.

HIGH OGRE
LEVEL: 40,000
EXTRA BOSS: Onizuka Dungeon

Its level was the same as that cyclops, which I had been lucky enough not to fight the other day. Like mice stumbling into a snake den, we found ourselves in a death trap.

◆❮◆

Yagami clucked his tongue in frustration at the high ogre that loomed before the party. A boss room should only exist on the last floor. That was common sense for any dungeon. That was why he'd use Enemy Detection so often to sense how close they were to the bottom.

How could this happen? Why would a boss room exist in the mid-levels? Especially one with an enemy that seemed less like a normal boss and more like a powerful extra boss?

No one was there to answer, but deep down, Yagami knew it: This was the dungeon's trap, plain and simple. The monster swarm and the conveniently empty tunnels were part of a plan. And he fell for it, hook, line, and sinker. Thanks to his lack of foresight, the party was stuck at the mercy of a level 40,000 monster—a beast more powerful than any of them.

Can we beat this monster by ourselves?

Yagami was the strongest adventurer in the group, but there was still a 26,000-level difference. Victory would be difficult to achieve, even with everyone working in lockstep, but they had to win if they wanted to escape.

"Leader!" shouted one of the members. They looked to Yagami expectantly, waiting for orders.

"Take battle formations!" he commanded. "Vanguard, don't focus on damage. Draw its attention. All sorcerers, provide cover while I deal the major blow! Healer, cast buff magic on everyone!"

"Sir, yes, sir!"

They were well-trained. Everyone nodded and assumed their positions around the high ogre. Yagami then remembered Amane Rin, standing behind him.

Based on his movement earlier, he could be useful in battle... but no. I can't.

He shook the idea out of his head. There was no way a kid had the power to take on a level 40,000 monster, let alone with a short sword at close range. It was plain to see Rin was no tank. Acting on the front line, where one mistake could cost him his life, was too much for the kid. Not to mention, he was brand new to the party, so he didn't know the formations like the others did.

That settled it. He had no business relying on some kid in a critical situation like this one.

Steadily, the heat of the battle rose. The tanks used their defensive skills to their utmost potential, not a single MP wasted, to stave off blows from the high ogre. They had to, or the monster's immense greatsword would wipe them out.

The knight and spearman searched for openings to slice the high ogre's ankles. The idea was to relieve the tanks of some of the pressure and limit the monster's movements.

A strangely tinny *clang* sounded when they stole a chance to strike.

"B-blades don't hurt it?!"

"Dammit! This monster's hard as a rock!"

A clangor rang out as they hit it again and again, even as their blades started to wear down and crack. Yagami wracked his brain, wondering how that could be when it wouldn't normally happen against any monster, even one this strong.

"It's using Harden!" he cried as he realized.

Harden was a skill that strengthened the body's durability. Tanks used it to defend the frontline. The high ogre must have the same power.

This was why high-level monsters were so nasty.

The higher their level, the more intricate and vexing their abilities became. He'd seen enough monsters to fill a zoo: snakes that spit acid, lizards rippling with fire, tortoises that could shake the earth...and a giant ogre that could harden its body, apparently. Defeating a monster with a specialty in defense wouldn't be easy, but that was no reason to lay down his weapon.

Yagami concentrated on conducting the chorus of battle. The vanguard's attacks bounced off the high ogre's skin, but they still dealt light injuries. No matter how tough a monster was, it was never invincible. If he could find an opening to attack with all his strength, that should be enough to defeat it.

Seconds later, the rhythm of the battle shifted, and the moment for attack arrived.

"Leader, *now*!" yelled the knight and spearman. After creating Yagami's opening with their brave attacks, they put some ground between themselves and the ogre.

Yagami gathered the mana inside his body and shouted, "Prominence Burst!"

Prominence Burst was a type of Advanced Magic, a fire spell that first spiraled into a ball, then blasted in a beam with enough strength to penetrate an iron wall. If it pierced the enemy's insides, it would spark a devastating explosion that destroyed the monster from the inside out.

Yagami held that ball of fire in his hands. He unleashed the spell, confident that not even the high ogre's hide could withstand it.

The high ogre snarled in anger when it noticed the spell flying its way, but it was too late. It couldn't evade in time. The stream of fire struck it dead center and sent debris flying through the room. The battle fell into a hush as everyone anticipated victory, but once the dust cleared—the high ogre stood unscathed.

"There's...no way...!" Yagami whispered.

It received a massive blow. How did the beast withstand that?

Did Prominence Burst not make contact? No, it did. It left slight scorch marks. But I landed a direct hit! So why did it only deal minimal damage?!

While he panicked internally, he held on to the expression of a leader, calm and collected. His eyes searched the high ogre's body until he spotted something.

Oh? There's a spot on its body, where the spell landed, but it's not a burn. It's like the ogre's skin changed to a darker shade of red. Everywhere else is lighter...

"It couldn't be," he hissed to himself, but he could only think one thing.

Can it actually change the strength of Harden on different sections of its body?!

If his hypothesis was correct, that would explain how it defended against even Prominence Burst. If it could concentrate the

Harden effect on its body to one location, its defensive capability would expand exponentially.

Adventurers couldn't use Harden like this. This was a monster-exclusive ability, and it was enough to render all of their attacks ineffective.

The situation only worsened from there. Like the monsters they encountered during their getaway, the high ogre appeared to have regenerative abilities. The scorch marks faded as he watched.

Dammit, this is trouble! It can defend with Harden and regenerate any scratch we inflict. Our only option is to inflict wounds faster than it can use Harden!

It was a plan, at least, but one he had no idea how to implement. All he knew was, if they didn't act now, they would die.

"Everyone, buy me more—"

The ogre's enraged roar cut him off as it prepared to charge *them.*

A tornado of turmoil, hopelessness, and terror tore a path through them. For the first time in a long time, the A-rankers remembered what it felt like to be an adventurer—no, a *person*—helpless in the face of danger.

Yagami pushed through the emotions buffeting him and shouted at his frightened, crumbling allies. "What are you doing?! Move! *Get away from it!*"

His voice didn't reach them. Their minds had submitted to the threat of the high orc. The monster swung its weapon down with a force powerful enough to obliterate everyone here, including the room itself.

Thud.

Desperate to buy the others time, the tanks moved forward to take the brunt of the attack, despite the threat of death. Uselessly, Yagami reached his hand toward them, but he was incapable of saving them from danger.

Then, time seemed to slow to the languid drip of molasses as Yagami witnessed something he couldn't believe:

A single young man gallantly dashed forward while the rest of them stood paralyzed.

What?!

Amane Rin, barely more than a boy and definitely not yet a man, launched himself at the high ogre with a silver longsword in hand.

"Wait, Amane!" Yagami blurted. "Don't throw your life away!"

He had no idea how Amane Rin could bring himself to move in this situation, but his body was far too small and insignificant to go against a level 40,000 monster.

The high ogre's unstoppable greatsword raced toward him.

Moments before rushing the high ogre, Rin was deep in thought. He watched from afar as Yagami and the rest of his party fought the high ogre.

The high ogre was level 40,000. His level was around 17,000, so the high ogre was a little more than double his level. Fundamentally, he understood this was the strongest monster he'd ever battled.

The level difference was wider than the gap between the lightning beast and himself, which had been sizable in and of itself. Not to mention, he was prepared for the lightning beast fight because of the Complete Recovery Potion and Magic Rebound Medicine he'd received as quest rewards. The system itself had granted him what he needed for the victory, narrow as said victory was.

This time was different. The high ogre was an irregular enemy that seemed placed in this dungeon by a malevolent hand. If Rin did everything in his power to spar with this monster, his true abilities would be revealed, and there was no guarantee that his everything would be enough.

He convinced himself that entrusting the fight to Yagami and the others, given their battle experience, was the right decision to make. He settled for watching them from a distance. It was only when Yagami's powerful magic failed to defeat the high orc and the rest of the party started to collapse that he reconsidered.

Yet... was clinging to his secret worth risking their lives?

He rejected the idea immediately. His secrets were worth *nothing* when people were in danger.

What am I here for if not for this?

The answer was crystal clear. He was there to fight challenging enemies, to struggle, and to climb ever higher in power. He wouldn't let the opportunity go.

"Nameless," he said.

The sword—a tool crafted to defeat intimidating enemies— manifested in his hand. He sprinted toward the high orc as it brought its greatsword down.

"Wait, Amane! Don't throw your life away!" someone shouted after him.

Rin didn't hear it. His mind was focused on the high orc's movements as he closed in on the speed of sound, the force of his steps powerful enough to crack the stone floor of the dungeon. With the cry of a fierce warrior, he swung Nameless up to counter the greatsword.

The blades clashed and scattered sparks. They strained against each other, evenly matched, until their swords clattered apart.

The others gaped with shock.

"How..."

"He *repelled* the greatsword?!"

The impact was forceful enough to repel everyone's fear and replace it with amazement. The high orc was no exception. It squinted down at Rin as if perplexed that such a tiny body could emit so much power.

Rin's reaction was different. From the observations he'd made on the sidelines, he understood the high ogre's unique abilities and how to combat them. The conditions he needed were met.

He stared the high ogre in its pitch-black eyes and promised, "I'll make a meal out of you."

The stage was set—as the stunned onlookers watched on, their grand battle began.

CHAPTER 4

DEVOURING THE STRONG

RIN FELT DEVOID of fear despite the beast of a monster looming over him.

When he fought the orc general, he had to suppress his emotions and stick to his hit-and-retreat strategy to come out on top. This time, he didn't need a cautious battle plan. In fact, he didn't need a battle plan at all.

His new power could overwhelm the high ogre completely.

"Time Zero!"

He blinked out of existence. Only the afterimage of his blade was visible as he slashed at the high ogre. It bellowed and swung its greatsword as if to drive away a pesky insect. Rin was already gone, having teleported to his next location.

"You sure you wanna try that again?" Rin taunted. "You won't activate Harden in time."

Fearful of Rin's power, the high ogre focused on shifting Harden to defend itself, but the attempt was futile. It couldn't see where Rin was until it was too late. None of its senses clued it in to Rin's location—until the sword decisively pierced its skin.

The high ogre roared in pain, but Rin didn't get cocky. Success was so close, close enough to taste. He attacked.

"What am I seeing?" Yagami whispered.

This kid wasn't even twenty years old, yet he was cutting the level 40,000 high ogre—the monster that pushed his entire party to the brink—down to size.

Strength, speed, spirit...there were *many* things Yagami could praise him for, but the most amazing was how he dodged the high ogre's attacks and then reappeared to slash its blind spots.

His *unique skill.*

One of his party members spoke up as they watched Rin fight the high ogre.

"Leader, who *is* this guy? I heard he was over level 10,000, but that doesn't explain those moves!"

Yagami didn't answer. He wasn't ignoring his guildmate. He was too deep in thought to notice the question.

Nineteen years old. One year of adventurer experience. Someone the guild master had his eye on. And *teleportation.*

One year ago, he heard rumors around the adventurer circles about a unique skill like that. Rin must be that skill's owner. If he was right, he could understand why this young man was special, and why the guild master would recruit him. Still, he couldn't grasp *how* Rin could earn so many levels! He'd only become an adventurer at eighteen, hadn't he?

Even if the math didn't add up, Amane Rin reached this tier *somehow*. Could his method help him outpace the young woman Yagami respected so much...?

That's impossible!

Yagami, who knew a piece of what made her special, didn't believe anyone could surpass her. Nevertheless, the heated battle before his eyes was so unlikely that it shook his faith. Amane Rin's strength was real.

I'll watch him carefully until I know the truth.

Reason and instinct dueled within him as fiercely as Rin dueled the high ogre. Watching this fight would decide exactly which side would win.

While anxiety and confusion still hung over the party members, a giddiness rippled through them as the climax of Rin's battle with the high ogre approached.

He'd easily landed over one hundred strikes. He only slowed when he recognized the renewed defensiveness of the ogre's hide.

Any defensive maneuver limited to a specific area wouldn't work on him. Increasing its overall defense to stave off *some* of the damage was better than nothing.

Returning Harden to its original stat, huh? Not a bad choice, but...

Time Zero allowed Rin to attack relentlessly. It was too late for this monster to depend on such a cheap trick. He had cornered it.

"Greed."

The command summoned his short sword Greed, gleaming crimson, into his left hand. Rin had considered absorbing magic from Yagami to pull off his battle plan, but he realized now that he didn't need it.

Definitively, he stabbed the high ogre's largest wound—now barely defended by Harden—with Greed's hungry blade.

"You've had your fun," he told the monster. "Release!"

The only spell that remained within Greed, the salamander's fire, unleashed inside the high ogre's body.

The ogre howled in agony as the fire rushed through its organs and burned it from the inside out. Based on the sounds tearing out of the monster's throat, the pain was excruciating. Fire burst like blood from the many wounds gouged into its torso.

Rin worried that a level 10,000 salamander's fire might not work on a level 40,000 creature, but Harden couldn't protect it from the inside, so the damage it dealt was substantial.

"Time's up," he said.

Rin teleported back to Yagami and the rest of the party, away from the ogre. Would they need to strike its wounds before it could regenerate? Rin felt their questioning gazes prickle his back.

They were right to wonder. Chain attacks with Time Zero were powerful, but all the teleporting made it difficult to put force into his attacks. The only way to gather real momentum for his final blow was to reach maximum speed. He blasted toward the ogre once again, his shoulders set. This monster wouldn't go down without a fight.

There was only one way to describe a mere teenager who struck down such a great and terrible enemy.

"Giant Eater."

Despite his slight appearance, it was the perfect description for him and the silver longsword he wielded.

The system spoke into everyone's mind and confirmed that yes, what they witnessed was real. Proof of the end of the battle, and that it was *Rin* who overpowered the high ogre.

And with that...the show was over.

Once the high ogre went down, the system rang out in my mind.

"*You have defeated the extra boss.*"

"*Gained XP: Level increased by 1,683!*"

"*Dungeon takedown reward: Level increased by 100!*"

"*Extra boss takedown reward: Level increased by 200!*"

Altogether, the takedown rewards amounted to 300 levels, which was a hefty sum. A far cry from the experience I gained, though.

The system spoke again.

"*First-time challenger of this dungeon: Confirmed.*"

"*Extra boss takedown: Confirmed.*"

"*All challengers' HP remains above 50 percent: Confirmed.*"

"*Bonus reward: Great Shield of Isolation.*"

As soon as the system stopped speaking, a hefty shield and a single candy-shaped item manifested. I approached the two items and used Appraisal.

FORTIFYING MEDICINE

Strengthens the body and decreases damage by 30% for 60 seconds.

COOLDOWN: 10 minutes.

GREAT SHIELD OF ISOLATION

RECOMMENDED EQUIP LEVEL: 40,000

DEFENSE +40,000

Temporarily boosts Defense in the event of a physical attack or Resistance in the event of a magic attack. The wielder may share these boosted stats with anyone inside the designated range.

"Another set of powerful items," I said under my breath.

The Fortifying Medicine alone was shockingly powerful, and that one was probably the normal takedown reward! The bonus reward item—the Great Shield of Isolation—was the real showstopper.

To boost defensive stats and transfer them to nearby party members was an *exceptional* ability. Sadly, the recommended level and size of the shield was way too much for me. It was so big, a petite girl could hide her entire body behind it. I'd have a heck of a time wielding it even if I tried a sword-and-board build. Only a tank could make the best use of it, but I wasn't friends with any tanks.

Oh, wait!

I was so deep in thought about Appraisal's results that I forgot the party was with me. I slowly turned to them. Not one of them moved to hide the fact that they were gaping at me like dead fish. Even Yagami-san looked confounded and his mouth floundered.

"Amane, how did you...?"

His mouth snapped closed. He'd remembered that he wasn't supposed to dig into my abilities, and if the leader wouldn't ask me, the rest of the party sure wouldn't. At least, that's what the awkward silence that filled the room suggested.

I had to say something, and weak excuses wouldn't bail me out. How much should I reveal to explain *this* incident away?

Yagami-san spoke before I could. "I never expected you to surprise us *this much* in one day. You surprised me so much, it hurts. I could hardly believe my eyes back there." He paused. "Amane, let me ask you one question. I know you've been an adventurer for one year, but did you ever dive *before* then?"

I understood immediately what he was asking. He wanted to know whether I'd illegally done dives to level up before I became eligible at age eighteen.

"No," I assured him. "I didn't do anything like that."

Not that my level-up method was any less sneaky, but that was *my* secret.

Yagami-san closed his eyes. "All right. I won't pry, and I knew you'd say as much...plus anyone who acted outside the law wouldn't publicize their useless unique skill, would they?"

He said the latter half under his breath, just to himself.

Regardless, as a sharply trained adventurer with excellent senses, I heard it all.

Yeah, a smart guy like him, he was likely on the cusp of discovering my skill's true nature. I'd given up on hiding my teleportation abilities during the fight, so I couldn't complain. If he discovered that I could bypass the Span, that was a different story.

No normal adventurer with only one year of experience could defeat a level 40,000 monster. Anyone with well-honed instincts would come to the truth—like Rei had—if they really thought about it. I hoped they wouldn't. I didn't suspect Yagami-san and his party would do anything nefarious with my secret, but I still wanted to keep it close.

"...Hm?" I said.

While I was thinking, the whole party had ducked their heads into a bow.

"Amane, you saved this party not once, but twice. Thank you so much," Yagami-san said.

The others repeated his words of thanks. What the heck? It was super uncomfortable to have these A-rank adventurers bowing to me.

"Please, there's no need," I said. "Let's just figure out how to split the rewards."

"You're the one who contributed most to the boss takedown," Yagami-san said. "In fact, you almost did it solo. You should take all of the rewards."

"Um, you sure? I can't use this huge shield! I'd be happy to give it away."

"Unfortunately, our guild doesn't have anyone who can wield a shield with a recommended level of 40,000. You're welcome to sell it or give it to someone you know. The level reward was plenty for us."

Oh yeah. Everyone *did* gain levels. That was common sense, but I always went solo, so I totally forgot. Three hundred levels was a worthy haul for them too. If they were satisfied, I would look obstinate if I refused to accept it.

"All right," I conceded. "I'll take the two rewards. Also..."

Before I could continue, a diffused light enveloped us.

"The Return Zone's calling. We'll talk later," Yagami-san said. "Before that, we better take the great sword from the high ogre too."

While Yagami-san hurried the team to collect the rest of the spoils, the back of my neck prickled. I turned to find Shinonome-san staring at me with her eyes unfocused.

"Shinonome-san? Is something wrong?"

"Huh?!" She snapped out of her haze. "N-no, everything's totally fine. Sorry, I spaced out!"

"Uh, okay...?"

I could have accepted that had she not mumbled something else under her breath. "Yeah! I'm just spacing out because he looked kinda cool while he was fighting. I'd never seriously go after a younger guy."

Uh. That was not a bomb I wanted to touch, so I looked anywhere but her until the teleportation magic activated a few seconds later. We were pulled out of the dungeon together, ending our group dive.

AMANE RIN

LEVEL: 19,438   SP: 26,710

TITLES: Dungeon Traveler (10/10), Nameless Swordsman,
Endbringer (ERROR), Wiser Wise Man

HP: 152,650/152,650   MP: 25,700/41,730

ATTACK: 36,170   DEFENSE: 30,520   SPEED: 37,840

INTELLIGENCE: 30,180   RESISTANCE: 30,310   LUCK: 29,360

SKILLS: Dungeon Teleportation LV 22, Enhanced Strength LV MAX,
Herculean Strength LV MAX, Superhuman Strength LV MAX,
High-speed Movement LV MAX, Gale Wind LV MAX,
Revitalize LV 1, Purification Magic LV 1, Mana Boost LV MAX,
Mana Recovery LV 2, Enemy Detection LV 4, Evasion LV 4,
Status Condition Resistance LV 4, Appraisal, Item Box LV 8,
Conceal LV 1, Battle Barrier LV 2, Plunderer LV 1

CHAPTER 5

A REASON TO FIGHT

WE DISBANDED after the group dive with little fanfare. Before we parted, though, they thanked me again and promised not to speak a word about my true abilities. They also expressed hope that someone like me would officially join the guild.

I avoided giving a concrete answer, but once I got home, I gave the prospect some real thought. While Yagami-san was a little harsh at the start, not once during the dive was anyone lording their rank over me. At the very least, they seemed like decent people. The rest was a matter of whether membership brought value to me. I wasn't so sure yet.

They were Yoizuki's top party, but during the high ogre battle, *I* was the one with the upper hand. Since my skills were best suited to solo work, working with a team didn't appeal to me much—that included having them as backup.

If possible, I'd prefer to work with Claire. She worked at a *way* higher level than they did.

"How strong *is* Claire, anyway?" I wondered aloud to the living room ceiling.

I knew S-rank adventurers were top of the proverbial adventurer's food chain, but that was only general knowledge. I'd never seen her *really* fight. I could tell that the level-40,000 cyclops she'd felled was just a hint of her ability. I doubted she put more than an ounce of her power into that fight.

If I were honest with myself, she was the most interesting thing about Yoizuki Guild. I couldn't make a decision about joining until I saw what *she* could do.

"Probably ought to keep that to myself..."

"Oniichan, what're you muttering to yourself about?" Hana asked as she sat down across from me.

"Hey, Hana," I said.

It was late enough that she was in her pajamas. The red ribbon I gave her a few years ago usually held her hair in a ponytail, but now her hair lay long and glossy over her shoulders, slightly damp from the bath. It granted her a more graceful look compared to the bouncy, upbeat air she normally projected. Not that it mattered—both hairstyles were charming on her.

This was a good chance to tell her she'd been on my mind lately. I had a big question for her.

"Hana, do you want to join a guild?" I asked.

"A guild?" She canted her head to the side.

Hana knew about my power. I didn't need to skirt the subject around her, so I explained everything happening with Yoizuki

Guild, which included that the guild master knew I was the one who executed Yanagi.

Hearing that, her eyes widened, but I assured her they didn't plan to have me punished for it. They didn't see a need for it.

She placed a hand on her chest and sighed with relief. "Thank goodness!"

I continued, explaining that the guild recruited me as a provisionary member. After I relayed the story of today's dive, I finished by telling her that we should think about her future steps.

I couldn't take her diving with me forever. Aside from us needing the backing of a guild, she needed a party—allies, really—she could trust. That was the most optimal way for her to level up, and with her unique skill, I doubted Yoizuki would reject her.

"Rei and Yui are members of Yoizuki too," I added. "I think you'll find plenty of trustworthy friends."

"Yeah, I'm sure I would, and I'd be happy to join with them there. It's just..." Hana paused for a second. "Are *you* okay with joining? You're saying we'd both become members, and as much as it's good for me, a guild doesn't seem like it's that useful for you."

"Sure it is. Being in the same guild would make it easier to talk about or cooperate on dungeon stuff, and it's not like there aren't *any* goals Yoizuki can help me with."

Hana seemed convinced after that. "Guess I'll consider my future too. I did want to join a guild..."

"I'll ask the guild master to meet with us. I think you should go in to talk—"

As I spoke, the phone lying next to me began to ring. The screen lit up with an unfamiliar number. I didn't know who it could possibly be, but I decided to answer it.

"Hello?"

A clear voice crackled across the line. "This is Kisaragi. I'm sorry for calling out of the blue."

She was the last person I expected on the other end.

"*Claire?* What's going on?" I asked. "Hold up, did I give you my number?"

"My father gave it to me. I need to speak to you."

"What about, exactly?" What could she possibly want that required a phone call? The suddenness of her call freaked me out, but I let her continue.

"If it's okay with you, Amane-san, can you spare some time tomorrow?"

"Sure, I guess." Was she not going to tell me *why*?

"Great. We'll meet at this time and place..."

I jotted down a quick note about the time and meetup location. "Works for me," I said.

"Perfect. I'll see you tomorrow."

"Yeah, see you then." Once we ended the call, I looked back at Hana. "Sorry, it was rude to take a call in the middle of our conversation."

Uh-oh. Hana was glowering at me, way more than I expected.

"Oniichan," she growled. "Was that a *girl* on the phone?"

"Yeah. She's someone I know from Yoizuki."

"Oh *really* now? You two sounded pretty cozy. Wait!" she gasped. "Is seeing *her* the goal you mentioned...?" She seemed to retreat into her own world. A world of *delusion*, if you asked me.

"Hello! Hana, you in there?" I prompted, but she didn't reply.

Another weird misunderstanding was undoubtedly swirling around her brain, but whatever. I was too tired to pull her back to reality. It had already been a long day. I was glad it was finally over.

Claire was there when I arrived at our meetup location. She appeared relaxed in her snow-white dress and soft blue cardigan.

"Sorry, I guess I made you wait," I said.

"Good morning, Amane-san," she replied. "Do not worry. You arrived before our meeting time."

"Cool. So, you wanted to talk about something?"

"Correct. Let's talk over a table instead of standing around."

We entered a nearby café where I ordered a milk tea, and she ordered a café au lait. Our conversation stayed light, but once our drinks arrived at the table, Claire got down to business.

"First, I'd like to thank you for yesterday. Yagami-san told me the gist of what happened," she explained. "If you weren't there, they would've struggled to defeat the extra boss. You protected them, and I'm truly grateful for that."

"You're welcome, but..." I glanced around. "Should we discuss this in public?"

"I'm using a soundproofing skill, so no other customers will hear us. Put your mind at ease."

She said it so casually, but I was startled to hear she had a skill like that.

"Let's debrief about the dungeon dive itself," she continued. "After your group dive, Onizuka Dungeon was determined too difficult even for an A-rank party, so they sent me in solo to document the particulars. I thought it only fair to share my findings with you, since you were there."

"Oh, nice. I'm definitely curious." Plus, this information could help me grind Onizuka.

"I found that Onizuka has three abnormal points to it. The first point is that it emits mana with regenerative properties. Monsters with powerful magic stones have the ability to absorb that mana, which grants them a high likelihood of regenerating."

Now that she mentioned it, what I witnessed down there matched her first point perfectly.

"The second abnormality is the monster swarm that appears on floor thirty. It only spawns a horde of monsters to attack *if* you stay there for longer than ten minutes. Finally, the third abnormality: If you run from those monsters, the dungeon leads you to an irregular room that spawns an extra boss. It must be fought to escape. That's where you and the rest of the party encountered the level-40,000 high ogre."

I could sense a *but* there. I nodded at her expectantly.

"But...if you *don't* enter the boss room and choose to fight the monsters instead, they stop spawning once you defeat a thousand of them."

"...Did you test that yourself?"

"Yes," she replied, deadpan.

One thousand monsters ranging from level 10,000 to 20,000... Yikes, that gave me flashbacks to the Remote Magic Tower! I wanted to clutch my head just from thinking about it. To Claire, it probably felt like mowing down riffraff in a hack-and-slash game. The gap between us was undeniably huge.

She continued. "If you descend the floors without fighting the high ogre, you'll encounter the final boss on the sixtieth floor. There, a level-25,000 ogre will spawn as the normal dungeon boss. The only takedown reward is a Fortifying Medicine that reduces damage by 20 percent."

"Oh, but I got a medicine from the high ogre that cuts damage by 30 percent, so that's not the same reward description. I imagine the level-up reward is different too?"

Defeating the high ogre and the dungeon takedown rewards provided a combined 300-level boost. Beating an ogre would grant, what, one hundred levels?

I had another question, though.

"Maybe I'm prying, but isn't dungeon investigation disproportionate to your abilities? I can't imagine the rewards were worth getting stuck in a Span."

There weren't a ton, but Japan had dungeons worth more than a hundred levels upon defeat. *Those* seemed worth her time, hence the reason I questioned her motives.

Claire's eyebrows drew together a little as she frowned. Was she troubled? "That's my duty as a guild member. I'm fine with that, so I don't require your concern."

She said it as if she was reciting from memory.

"Right, no problem," I conceded. If she didn't want me to, I wouldn't pry any further. I lifted my cup and sipped my milk tea while it was still hot. "Is that all you wanted to talk about?"

"No, that was simply a brief show of thanks and a report. I *actually* asked you here for something else. It's a more personal matter." She sat straighter and met my gaze with a marksman's intensity. "Amane-san, may I ask *why* you became an adventurer?"

"You want my reason...?"

"Yes," she said with a nod. "When I heard the report about your defeat of the high ogre, I realized you were much stronger than I had anticipated. No normal adventurer grasps that kind of power at your age."

Said the pot to the kettle, but I wasn't going to interject. I kept listening.

"It's been two decades since dungeons first appeared and vastly changed our world. Humankind was granted great powers by the level system," she said. "At the time, we only knew of what we now call E-rank dungeons, but the resources inside of them were still valuable."

Claire withdrew several sizes of magic stones from an

invisible pocket in space and set them on the table. She must've used Item Box.

"Once we learned that we could use mana as an energy source, countries began harvesting efforts. Only a few hundred thousand people could retrieve magic stones from those E-rank monsters, but once higher-ranked dungeons manifested, their worth decreased. Nowadays, these are worth a few hundred yen at most." She gestured to her visual aids on the table.

"Yup, that's the reality, isn't it? Value's still trending down too," I said. "It takes becoming a C-rank adventurer to make a living, and the amount you make drops every few years."

That was why everyone around me told me to quit adventuring. Those without talent could never catch up, no matter how fast they leveled up. By the time they reached their goal, the value of dungeon resources would have changed, and their spoils would sell for as little as they always had. A goalpost that never stopped moving.

Dungeons had existed nearly since Claire and I were born, but the history of *our* world didn't amount to anything compared to the history of *the* world. The arrival of dungeons would ripple throughout history, well beyond our lifetimes.

Claire wasn't finished. "Common sense dictates that, considering the fixed level-up rewards and the Span, those who become adventurers now will never catch up to the veterans. The only people who can overcome that are those with promising unique skills. They soar over the drudgery of others and reach greater heights through luck."

Claire's hands tightened on her cup of coffee. Had someone accused her of that before? Something about her face told me she was recalling a memory.

"Many people say things like that about adventurers with unique skills, but I don't agree," she said. "I believe those adventurers suffer a great deal *because* of their power, yet they strive for greater heights nonetheless."

Her eyes blazed as she stared at me.

"That's why I'm so curious about you," she said. "If you have the power it takes to topple that high ogre, you must've struggled to get there. In essence, I am asking how you have not cracked under the immense pressure."

Her lovely blue eyes bore into me. How could I lie to someone so earnest? I wanted to answer her honestly.

"I..."

Slowly, I told Claire the same story I told Rei once upon a time—the story about why I became an adventurer.

That fateful day, Hana and I were on an errand when a dungeon collapse occurred nearby. The street flooded with monsters. We were about to die at the hands of a massive monster when a single adventurer rushed in to defeat it and save us. Staring up at his back in awe, I knew I wanted to be just like him. The memory was fuzzy nowadays, so I couldn't remember who he was, but what I *could* remember was the desire to grow up just like him—strong, capable of protecting strangers and loved ones alike. Money and proving myself were afterthoughts.

The *main* reason was that simple.

"...There's nothing more to it," I finished.

I kept the story concise. I was the minority among adventurers, most of whom were in it for fame and fortune. But I was hardly *alone*—others felt the same way.

What would Claire think of my story? I anxiously awaited her reaction.

"I think that's a wonderful reason," she said. Her smile was as gentle and light as the sound of piano music playing in another room. The unexpected beauty of it caught me off guard. In that moment, she seemed like the only person in the café.

"Yui-san and Rei-san have told me quite a bit about you," she added. "They say they're grateful for the help you've provided them, and the same goes for Yagami-san's party. Your goal is well on its way to being realized."

"You think so?"

"No, I *know* it. And once you do realize it, I hope you'll be..." She drew a sharp breath and shut her mouth as if catching herself.

"Something wrong?" I asked.

"Oh, no, not at all. Your drink is running low. Would you like another?"

"Nah, I'm good."

I gulped down the rest of my milk tea, though it had cooled as we talked. It seemed like Claire had said everything she wanted to say, so it was about time we parted ways, but...

"Can I ask you something?" I couldn't let her go without one more question.

"Yes, what is it?"

"What's *your* reason for becoming an adventurer?"

I was equally interested in her answer. Maybe it would offer a glimpse of her strength.

Claire's eyes widened, a stark contrast to her gentle smile when she heard my reason. The air in the café chilled somehow, cold like her eyes as they looked at me—or rather, looked past me. What she saw wasn't *here*.

Her pink lips moved slightly before she spoke.

"I'm here to protect *everything*," she answered. "That is my duty."

"Your...duty?"

Not a goal or a dream, but a *duty*? She said those words as if they weren't hers.

"Claire—"

"Or something along those lines," she rushed, cutting me off. "My reason isn't so different from yours."

I didn't reply: I didn't know *how* to. The opportunity to ask for more detail slipped away. The gentle atmosphere returned, though I sensed crystals of ice in the air, as if she was warding me off treading any further into her thoughts. An uncomfortable silence fell over us.

Claire was the one to slash through it. "Amane-san, thank you for meeting me here today. I'm glad we had this important discussion. Shall we go?"

She picked up the order ticket and rose. Why was her expression so lonely as she turned away? The urge to turn her around somehow surged through me.

"Wait, Claire."

"Yes?" she said, turning toward me.

Well, I was glad, but I didn't know what to say. After a weird pause that probably took a year off my life, I settled on my answer.

"Did you know that Wolfun version two will appear in Magidun next week?"

"...Come to think of it, I believe I'd like another cup of coffee."

"Oh—yeah! Me too."

Claire and I chatted up a storm about Wolfun for an hour before parting. I didn't go home right away. Instead, I traveled to Onizuka Dungeon. There were still too many unknowns about Onizuka, so it was closed off to normal adventurers, but I knew of no better place to level up for a guy like me. I decided to teleport inside from a location away from any nosy onlookers. It wasn't the most ethical thing to do, but desperate times called for desperate measures.

"Dungeon Teleportation!"

I teleported rapidly to floor thirty. Claire said the monster swarm would only spawn if an adventurer stayed on that floor for over ten minutes, but I didn't wait for that. I headed straight for the irregular extra boss room where the high ogre waited. Once

I entered, the doors behind me slammed shut and the muddy crimson body of the high ogre pushed out of the wall. It roared to high heaven.

"I'm glad to see you're ready for round two," I said to it. "Thanks."

I drew Nameless and faced the high ogre. Unlike yesterday, Greed wasn't stocked with stolen magic. I had to beat this monster with my strength alone, but I wouldn't flinch. Beating Onizuka granted me a 2000-level boost, spiked my stats, and loaded me with enough SP for a few new skills. With plenty of tricks up my sleeve, there was no way I'd lose, even without magic.

"Buckle up!"

My second battle with the high ogre immediately revved into high gear.

Tens—even *hundreds* of flashes of my blade sliced through the air. Each strike compounded the next until they totaled one huge impact that split the high ogre's tough hide, deeper and deeper. It growled in frustration as it tried to counter me.

"Way too slow!"

I used Time Zero to dodge its attacks and land even more hits, flitting around its body like a mosquito. The high ogre's coarse strength remained a threat, but if I kept my cool and evaded its clumsy counters, I could dodge it all night. Time Zero was perfect against giant monsters like this one. Monsters with magic attacks like the salamander and the gryphon required more strategy, but the high ogre specialized in physical attacks and defensive magic.

Thanks to that, defeating it took about a minute. Without Greed and a spell to help me out, I couldn't beat my first record, but it was close enough for me.

The flow of the fight continued as I reliably whittled down its HP. Soon, I found an opening and swung Nameless. The silver blade sliced a huge gash in the high ogre's weakened chest and destroyed the magic stone inside. It disintegrated.

The system dinged, announcing my victory and a huge chunk of experience.

"Gained XP: Level increased by 1,213!"

"Dungeon takedown reward: Level increased by 100!"

"Extra boss takedown reward: Level increased by 100!"

I checked my status screen. I'd activated Superhuman Strength, Gale Wind, and Time Zero at the same time, so the MP drainage was pretty rough, but I had some mana still to spare.

"I'm just getting started," I said. After the dungeon's teleportation spell transported me to the Return Zone, I reentered the dungeon's depths once again.

"Wait. I *could* beat it again, but I should check my skills first."

I opened my stats display and found the skills I'd obtained yesterday ahead of my return to diving in Onizuka.

Endurance LV MAX: Defense +3,000
Adamantine LV 5: +50% to Defense (COSTS 10 MP PER SECOND)
Enhanced Spirit LV MAX: Resistance +3,000
Tenacity LV 5: +50% to Defense

When I was home last night, I'd leveled up skills that elevated my Defense or Resistance in some way, like how High-speed Movement and Gale Wind elevated Speed.

"Can't rely on Time Zero and Battle Barrier all the time, after all."

Sure, they were superior, special skills. I could spam Time Zero to evade attacks, and Battle Barrier reduced damage to almost zero, but their positives hid negatives of their own.

"Time Zero is only helpful *inside* a dungeon, not to mention it drains MP like no other. If I'm not careful, I could lose a thousand MP in a second. I gotta get used to fighting without it."

I knew too well that battles sometimes occurred aboveground. Monsters could escape from dungeons, and if they got an edge on me there, things could go downhill *quick*. I needed to prepare for every scenario.

"Battle Barrier will come in handy when I can't use Time Zero, but there's downsides to relying on it too."

Battle Barrier carried a one-minute cooldown. It didn't seem like much at first glance, but during a serious fight, life and death was measured in seconds. If I ever found myself unable to evade after my barrier was breached, I would be a sitting duck until I reactivated it.

Unexciting as they were, that's why I went with defensive skills this time around. I would rather have gone without them and picked a more fun option, but I treated it like buying life insurance and signed up.

"Sorry, Battle Barrier. Now, what about Time Zero? Should I challenge the high ogre without using it? I've fought it twice, so I think I've figured out its attack patterns anyway. Yeah!"

My mind made up, I set off for the thirtieth floor. After following the winding path, I entered battle with the high ogre for a third time. As usual, in terms of raw power it had me beat, but I relaxed and watched for openings. Even without Time Zero, my measured battle strategy allowed me to deal damage in small, consistent increments.

Three minutes after the fight began, the high ogre fell over dead.

"Gained XP: Level increased by 1,022!"

"Dungeon takedown reward: Level increased by 100!"

"Extra boss takedown reward: Level increased by 200!"

I listened, a little awed. "The XP reward is always so high..."

The conditions to spawn this extra boss were easy to fulfill, so I gained the dungeon takedown reward *and* extra boss takedown reward totaling 300 levels each time. Plus, since the high ogre's level was much higher than mine, the experience I earned for its defeat spiked my level even further. One Onizuka run boosted my level at a rate normal adventurers would kill for—and thanks to Dungeon Teleportation, I could loop it several times per day.

My unique skill was a real blessing. It was valuable not only for traveling the dungeon and fighting, but for getting me inside the dungeons with the best rewards over and over! Thanks to its awakening, I was leveling up faster than anyone imagined.

Naturally, I went for more dives and jumped so many levels, I even surprised myself.

I continued my efforts the next day. The extreme improvements to my stats made defeating the high ogre easier each time.

"Gained XP: Level increased by 423!"

"Dungeon takedown reward: Level increased by 100!"

"Extra boss takedown reward: Level increased by 200!"

As I entered battle with the high ogre yet again, Claire's words from the other day surfaced in the back of my mind. Two things she said stuck out to me. The first was what she said after I gave my reason for becoming an adventurer.

"Yui-san and Rei-san have told me quite a bit about you. They say they're grateful for the help you've provided them, and the same goes for Yagami-san's party. Your goal is well on its way to being realized," she'd said.

"...You think so?" I'd replied.

"No, I *know* it. And once you do realize it, I hope you'll be..."

That's where she cut herself off. What was she about to say? What did she hope would happen once I became strong enough to protect the people I loved?

"Gained XP: Level increased by 253!"

"Dungeon takedown reward: Level increased by 100!"

"Extra boss takedown reward: Level increased by 200!"

The second thing she said made me even more curious. When I asked her what *her* reason was, her response was peculiar.

"I'm here to protect *everything*. That is my duty."

She didn't call it her goal or her dream: Claire called it her duty. I didn't know why. My only theory was that she might feel an obligation to protect people who didn't have that power, something conventional like that. *I* felt that way.

"Gained XP: Level increased by 87!"

"Dungeon takedown reward: Level increased by 100!"

"Extra boss takedown reward: Level increased by 200!"

I still had no idea why she sought power or why she possessed the power she did. Could I find out if I reached S-rank?

Until I met Claire, all I strived for was power. I couldn't say why I was suddenly thinking so deeply about someone else, but she occupied so many of my thoughts, nonetheless. I had a hunch about one thing: I wouldn't figure out why she lived rent free in my head unless I caught up to her.

So, I leveled up.

"Gained XP: Level increased by 13!"

"Dungeon takedown reward: Level increased by 100!"

"Extra boss takedown reward: Level increased by 200!"

Six days of solo takedowns. Fourteen total runs ending in battles with the extra boss. Once more, the high ogre stood before me and raised its greatsword high.

Nowhere to run and nowhere to hide. I raised Nameless in the same way as my opponent, prepared to take its hit head-on.

We both roared like beasts and swung our swords with flashes of metallic light. The match was decided instantaneously—the sharpened blades clanged together and the greatsword snapped, unable to endure the pressure from my own. The broken blade helicoptered across the room. With so much force behind it,

Nameless plunged forward and slashed into the high ogre's torso, splitting its magic stone.

"*Gained XP: Level increased by 8!*"

"*Dungeon takedown reward: Level increased by 100!*"

"*Extra boss takedown reward: Level increased by 200!*"

The system didn't stop its dry speech.

"*You have reached this dungeon's maximum number of allotted victories.*"

"*Bonus Reward: Level increased by 500!*"

"*You will no longer receive rewards for defeating this dungeon.*"

"That's the end of my time here, then," I said slowly.

Onizuka Dungeon...was finished.

AMANE RIN

LEVEL: 39,830   **SP:** 34,710

TITLES: Dungeon Traveler (10/10), Nameless Swordsman, Endbringer (ERROR), Wiser Wise Man

HP: 312,660/312,660   **MP:** 85,640/85,640

ATTACK: 73,770   **DEFENSE:** 62,450   **SPEED:** 77,720

INTELLIGENCE: 61,520   **RESISTANCE:** 61,810   **LUCK:** 61,030

SKILLS: Dungeon Teleportation LV 29, Enhanced Strength LV MAX, Herculean Strength LV MAX, Superhuman Strength LV MAX, Endurance LV MAX, Adamantine LV MAX, High-speed Movement LV MAX, Gale Wind LV MAX, Enhanced Spirit LV MAX, Tenacity LV MAX, Revitalize LV 1, Purification Magic LV 1, Mana Boost LV MAX, Mana Recovery LV 2, Enemy Detection LV 4,

Evasion LV 4, Status Condition Resistance LV 4, Appraisal, Item Box LV 8, Conceal LV 1, Battle Barrier LV 5, Plunderer LV 1

DUNGEON TELEPORTATION LV 29

REQUIRED MP: 1 MP × Distance (meters)

CONDITIONS: Teleportation can occur in all dungeons.

TELEPORTATION DISTANCE: Maximum 1,000 meters.

ACTIVATION TIME: 0.2 seconds × distance (meters)

SCOPE: User and user's belongings.

SUB-SKILL: Time Zero

Paying 100 MP allows the user to teleport instantly within a 20-meter radius.

Dungeon Teleportation LV 29 → LV 30 (SP NEEDED: 50,000)

THE WORLD'S FASTEST
LEVEL UP

CHAPTER 6

TURNING POINT

WITH ONIZUKA MAXED OUT, I checked my stats again.

"I can't believe my level more than doubled in just one week." My growth was so wild, I couldn't *begin* to justify it to a normal adventurer.

Next, I reviewed my skill list, where I saw Battle Barrier LV 5 and Dungeon Teleportation LV 29.

"Battle Barrier is normal so far, wanting the usual bump in SP each time. It made sense to get it to LV 5 then switch priorities to Dungeon Teleportation but...I still don't have enough SP to reach LV 30."

I'd shoveled SP into it until Dungeon Teleportation reached LV 29 but didn't see much difference in its abilities. There was no need to get upset over it, though. The same thing happened between each ten-level increment, other than the surprise at LV 21. I shrugged and focused on something else.

"Each skill level increase required 10,000 SP, but LV 30 requires *50,000 points*...what the heck is it gonna do with that much SP?"

Something as awesome as Time Zero, right? It's just gotta be something that good.

On second thought, I would be in for a world of hurt if I let my hopes fly that high. Dungeon Teleportation grew as unpredictably as a weed on the side of the road. It was dangerous to put too much faith in LV 30.

"I need to stop overthinking this," I decided. "I'll have the answer soon enough."

More specifically, I'd have my answer in about two days. I only needed 15,000 SP to reach the 50,000 SP cost. Thinking about it put a pep in my step.

I chatted with Hana over dinner that night.

"Hey, remember the guild I mentioned? They can make time to talk to you tomorrow afternoon. Think you can make it?" I asked.

"Yeah! So long as it's in the afternoon."

"Oh, plans in the morning?"

"I'm gonna hang out with Yui-senpai and Rei-senpai." She paused to think. "I know! Why don't you come with us?"

"Me again?"

I asked where and she named a shopping mall in the city center. It was close to Yoizuki's headquarters, so not a bad place to meet. This way, we wouldn't need to regroup before heading over.

"You should probably ask them before inviting me, though," I warned.

"I don't think they'd mind, but gimme a sec."

She pulled out her phone and typed out a quick text. Replies came immediately.

"Witness!" she said, brandishing the screen like she'd drawn Excalibur. It displayed a group chat between the three of them, which I had no idea existed.

Gee, thanks for the invite.

Yui had responded with an enthusiastic, *Ooooo, fine by me!* and Rei had sent a sticker with big letters that said *'OK'* and *'YAY!'* The way their personalities shone through their messages was kind of funny.

"Well, guess I might as well come along," I said.

"Yes, you *should*!"

Hana giggled excitedly and texted to let them know I'd be there. All of a sudden, my schedule for the next day was solidly booked.

Once we arrived at the mall, Hana peered around and hummed in thought. "I don't think Yui-senpai and Rei-senpai are here yet."

"We're kinda early," I said.

It wasn't long before we heard Yui's voice. "Hana-chan and Rin-senpai!" she called. "Good morning!"

She practically bounced over on a cloud, her long light hair swaying behind her. Her bright eyes had a way of drawing in everyone around her. From her expression to her stylish clothes, her energy screamed 'cutesy girl,' but, you know, in a good way.

Rei arrived next. Her straight hair was styled and the ends hovered just above her shoulders. "Long time no see, everyone," she said calmly.

Appearance-wise, Rei was cute too, but *pretty* was probably the better word for her style. Ask any passerby and I bet they'd say the same thing. Though if they actually talked to her, they'd see that she was a little absent-minded, but her immature side popped out easily, and her cuteness wasn't lacking by any means... What was I saying?

"I haven't seen you two since snacks at the guild," I said. "How've you been?"

"Good! I was *sooooo* glad to hear you'd be here today!" Yui answered first.

"I as well," Rei added.

"Yeah? I'm glad to see you too," I said. They didn't seem to say it out of politeness, so I relaxed a bit.

"Now that we're all here, let's get going!" Hana said impatiently, taking the lead.

I hurried after her. "Hana, if you walk that fast, we might get separated."

"Don't worry, oniichan! It isn't crowded today."

Just five minutes later, we got separated. Yui and I somehow found ourselves with Hana and Rei nowhere to be seen.

"I didn't think we'd *actually* lose each other," I said.

Yui laughed. "All we did was check out a shop window for *one second* and they vanished without us!"

Hana and Rei were both the type to take the lead, so they didn't notice us stop.

"Hana said we're here for fun more than actually buying anything, so we can just window shop," I said. "Still, I didn't expect to split up so fast."

"Ha, right? I'm surprised too. This doesn't usually happen when I hang out with my other friends." She scratched her cheek, visibly puzzled.

She was such a social person that I imagined her with a boatload of friends. I could picture her on hangouts like these all the time, laughing up a storm.

Hana had a lot of friends too, but when I thought about it, she didn't see them that much. Without our parents around to help us, she spent a lot of her spare time on housework. That sucked, but she had *some* time for herself. Though...if I was home, she was usually home too. Then again, I didn't really know what she did daily since I became a full-time adventurer.

As for Rei, I couldn't fully guess. I thought she was the closed-off type at first, but we were similar, weren't we? Kind of paradoxical. We both liked our solitude but also liked having friends.

Not that I intended to analyze Rei *too* deeply.

"They left us behind, so why don't we go somewhere too?" I suggested.

"Really? Shouldn't we wait for them?"

"I sent them a text saying we can regroup later, since waiting is a waste of time. How about we poke around together?"

Yui's eyes almost crossed for a second, but she shook out of it swiftly and smiled wide. "S-sure! I'd love to!"

As we strolled around the various shops, we meandered toward our meeting spot with Hana and Rei. Along the way, we tried on sunglasses and necklaces at an accessory shop, where a salesperson thought we were a couple. When I denied it, Yui glared at me. It wasn't my fault other people misunderstood us! Overall, though, we had fun.

As we walked on, Yui began to tell me about her family.

"Huh, so you also have a little sister?" I asked.

"Yeah, and that's it. Just us two sisters."

Something about her slotted into place when she said that. Sure, she was a little clueless here and there, but I sensed she was a top-notch big sister.

"What's she like?"

"Um, she's quieter than me. Her health is kind of crummy, so when the seasons change, she tends to get sick and miss school. I think that's part of why she's so quiet...but she's still really sweet! Super lovable too!"

"It sounds like you care a lot about her."

"Yeah, I do!" She nodded, beaming.

I totally understood how it felt to have such a special little sister. Seeing the pride Yui had in her sister made my heart feel full too.

"Oh!" Yui exclaimed. "I have a picture of her. Wanna see?"

"Can I?"

"Of course."

She handed me her phone, which showed a picture of her posed beside a younger girl with a neat bob. Her demeanor looked docile, especially when compared to Yui's.

"Her name is Sae. She's in her third year of middle school. Isn't she cute?"

"Yeah," I said as I passed her phone back. "She's just as cute as her big sister."

"Meep?!"

"Huh?" What? Why had Yui reacted so weirdly? Her face was red as a boiled crab. As I tried to puzzle out the problem, she pouted and grumbled at me.

"R-Rin-senpai!" she scolded. "You can't say stuff like that out of nowhere! I bet you say those things to Rei-chan and Hana-chan too!"

"What's the problem? I'm not following."

"Go back over your own words and think again!"

"Okay."

I couldn't ignore her, given how insistent she was, so I backtracked what we'd said word for word. First, she showed me the picture of her cute little sister, Sae-chan, and then she asked me if I thought she was cute, and I agreed. She was cute in a similar way to Yui. I mean, I only said the truth—

Wait. *Now* I saw why her face was so red. The way I phrased it...I admitted she was cute, didn't I?

"Uh, I didn't mean it like *that*...but I also *didn't* not mean it like that?" I scrambled. Denying it felt like the wrong way to go too. Should I lie or be honest? I *did* think Yui was cute. That's the reason I said it in the first place!

If Rei was the unobtainable beauty up in her tower, Yui was the sort of open girl who was kind to everyone, including the boys in her class who would get the wrong idea and end up heartbroken over it. How would you even sum up that sort of girl?

Okay, I was getting off track. Back to the topic at hand.

A gloom fell between us. Neither of us knew what to say. Lucky for us, someone else appeared.

"I'm sensing tension right out of a romcom," Rei said.

Hana turned her nose up. "We take our eyes off you for *one second* and this is what you do?"

Both of them wore sulky expressions. Yui and I scrambled for excuses, but internally, I was grateful the two of them showed up to break the awkwardness.

After that, the four of us stuck together and wandered the mall until eleven a.m., when we stopped for an early lunch at the food court. We secured some seats, then Hana and Yui went to find their food first while Rei and I stayed behind.

"Rin," she said.

"Yeah?"

She scooted next to me and leaned in close enough that people around us couldn't hear. "I need to talk to you about something—alone."

"Alone?"

"Yes." She nodded. "It's been a while since you rescued me, and I'm curious how much stronger you've become."

"You mean, what's my level?"

Her eyes were earnest. I didn't know *why* she wanted to know, but she already knew about Dungeon Teleportation. No reason to hide the truth from her.

I held up four fingers. Rei's eyes widened as she understood that I'd reached level 40,000.

"You grew *that* much? Wow... Speaking of, has anyone else learned about your power?"

"Hana knows everything. It was the right time. Also, the guild master, Claire, and Yagami-san's party know what I can do in battle. Just a matter of time until they learn the extent of Dungeon Teleportation's secrets, probably."

"Oh. So many people already know," she replied, her face falling. She let a few seconds of silence pass. "Remember when I said I wanted to dive a dungeon with you again someday?"

"Of course."

"I truly meant it. I've gone with Hana and Yui, but it's different with you. I want to be helpful to *you*. I want to be someone you can depend on," she said. "But as hard as I've worked since then, I've barely surpassed level 1,000. I doubt I'll ever give you real support."

"...Rei."

She looked so depressed, that was all I could manage. What else could I say, when she was basically correct? My level had already blown *so* far past hers. Even if I dove with her for training, we couldn't seriously tackle the same dungeon together anymore.

Dungeon Teleportation blessed me with the power to level up faster than anyone else, but it also put distance between me and others. I pursued strength because it was my goal, but I never considered who I would leave behind.

I recalled what Claire said to me a week ago—the only adventurers who became world-class were the ones with promising unique skills. They soared over the drudgery of others and reached great heights through luck.

I'd fought so many powerful enemies, sometimes clawing my way back from the brink of death. I felt like the power I'd gained by surviving *was* earned. On the other hand, if it weren't for Dungeon Teleportation's unique abilities, I never could've gotten this far. From my lofty position, what was there to say to her? I had no idea, but I couldn't say *nothing*.

I put my hand on her head. When words failed me, this was all I knew how to do.

"Rin?"

"Sorry. You can push me away if you don't like it."

She looked a little surprised, but then she smiled softly.

"I don't mind." She rested her head on my shoulder.

I stayed silent and let her. Rei's regrets wouldn't disappear with this. We both knew that, but in that moment we shared how much we respected and cared for each other. I was sure of it.

"Just when I looked away *again*! Oniichan, I swear!" Hana grumbled.

"I *knew* Rei-chan would try something similar...no, she did *more*!"

Rei and I jolted apart and froze.

After that brief disturbance, we walked toward Yoizuki. Yui and Rei had guild business to attend to, so they tagged along.

On the way, I caught sight of a familiar face.

"Yagami-san? Ah, the whole gang's here."

The other members of his party were nearby. Yagami-san, at the helm as always, turned to look at me.

"Amane. Kurosaki and Kasai too?" he said, then turned to Hana. "Who is she?"

"My little sister. Hana, these people are members of the Yoizuki Guild."

"Oh! I'm Amane Hana. Nice to meet you!"

"Yagami. The feeling's mutual," he replied. "I heard you were bringing someone to introduce to the guild, Amane. Your sister, huh?" He nodded like a fishmonger appraising a fresh catch.

"What's everyone up to?" I asked. "Your whole party's here, but aren't you subject to the Span today?"

"We're diving tomorrow, so we did some light drills at the Dungeon Association's training center. We're on our way back from that."

"Ah, gotcha."

As we talked, Shinonome-san peered out from behind Yagami-san. "Way to go, Amane-kun," she said. "You've got three cuties on your tail."

"Please, don't put it like that..."

"Tee hee! I'm kidding. Since you're here, why don't we go to the guild together?"

I didn't see why not, so we joined them. Along the way, we passed a location I was well acquainted with, but it wasn't like I remembered. This was where Kenzaki Dungeon was supposed to be.

"Is this really...?" I started.

"Yeah," Shinonome-san said. "The remnants of Kenzaki. It's a shadow of its former self, isn't it?"

She was right. It was just a normal park. She gazed upon it and said quietly, "It's so weird how the location returns to the way it was before, like the dungeon never existed."

"Yeah, it's strange," I whispered, shaken for some reason.

When dungeons appeared around the world, they left no trace of the people, animals, or things that were there before. Conversely, when the dungeons vanished, their locations reverted to the states they were originally in. Specialists had named the phenomenon "replacement," but they didn't know *why* it happened.

Whatever the cause, Kenzaki Dungeon's location was replaced with the expansive park it used to be, not a change as far as the eye could see. It was always a beautiful park, famous for its lush flowers and greenery. It was currently packed with happy park-goers who hadn't seen it in years.

"You two dozing off back there? Hurry it up!" Yagami-san said.

"Oh! Whoopsie!" Shinonome-san chimed.

I pushed the mysteries of dungeons to the back of my mind. We started for Yoizuki again, until something stopped me dead. Ice water flooded my veins, and I felt like someone's eyes were piercing through me. The last time I felt something like this...was Yanagi.

I know this feeling.

It was malice—no, it was *bloodlust*.

I braced my suddenly shaking legs and inspected the area around us. I didn't see anything suspicious. Hana, Yui, and Rei glanced at me in confusion.

"Oniichan? What hap—"

She cut herself off with a gasp. Swampy, oozing darkness swallowed the ground and spread beneath our feet. That darkness captured me, Hana, *everyone*, even the park itself. People in the crowd began to scream.

"What is this stuff?!" someone shrieked.

I knew. There was no doubt what was happening, but why *now*? This wasn't possible! My head scrambled with the static of doubt and panic, but I had to act.

"Everyone, run!" I shouted.

"Run, you'll get pulled in!" Yagami-san echoed.

Yet none of us could escape. *I* might've managed it if I was fast, but Hana was here. *Civilians* were here. Even if I had wanted to escape, time was up. The darkness quivered like a waiting throat, then swallowed.

I lifted my legs and struggled to stay above ground, but it

sucked me down further and further. Soon, all I could do was utter one measly curse.

"Damn...it! No!"

No one replied.

We were dragged, together, into a dungeon outbreak.

For several seconds, a weightless, floating sensation enveloped me—until it abruptly dissipated, leaving me hovering several feet above the hard, uneven ground characteristic of dungeons.

"Whoa," I breathed as I landed, careful to stay upright.

The other adventurers around me also landed with their feet solidly on the ground, but the civilians without stats fell flat on their backs and faces. At least no one seemed seriously injured, so that was a small relief.

Rei approached my side. "Rin, is this what I think it is?"

"If you're thinking dungeon outbreak, definitely—no doubt."

"That doesn't make sense. Dungeons rarely spawn from the ruins of another dungeon, and if they do, at least a year goes by before it happens."

Rei was right, and that wasn't the only strange thing. After years of dungeon research, researchers hadn't found a way to stop dungeons from spawning, but they *had* found ways to manipulate *where* they spawned—in places with few people and buildings. Thanks to that, no incidents of people being lost to dungeon outbreaks occurred in the last few years.

Until us.

Ugh. My new life of irregular occurrences was giving me a headache...

"I don't know why it grabbed us, but I bet a monster will pop out of this dungeon at any moment. We should gear up," I said.

"Got it," Rei said with a nod.

We were just hanging out, so were dressed casually. Rei and I used Item Box, which formed a glow around us. Once the light vanished, our gear was left in its place. I turned to Hana and Yui.

"Yui, do you have Item Box?" I asked.

"Yep! I got it recently."

"Nice, that helps. Hana doesn't have one yet."

"I still have a simple coat I used to wear. Hana should be able to equip it," Rei offered.

"Thank you, Rei-senpai!" Hana said.

Every other adventurer present had the same idea, as they'd also changed into their battle gear. We'd finished a necessary first step. As for the next step, I started toward Yagami-san. He would know best.

"Rin-senpai, watch out!" Yui screamed.

Before her voice finished echoing, a black mass leapt out from the shadow beneath my feet. It swung an umbral knife at my throat.

"Don't waste my time," I hissed.

I summoned Greed and swung, cutting the mystery monster in half. It crumbled away. From the way my blade hitched as it passed through it, I guessed it was around level 20,000. That meant this dungeon was at least A-rank.

"Huh?" Yui said. "What just..."

She blinked like someone was shining a light in her eyes and she couldn't see clearly. Yui didn't know the extent of my abilities, so yeah, she *would* be surprised.

"Hana, Rei, keep an eye on Yui."

"Okay!"

"Got it."

It reassured me to know they'd stop Yui from freaking out. I used Enemy Detection to confirm no other monsters were hiding inside the room, then made my way to Yagami-san and his party. They all wore hangdog expressions.

"Hey, Amane," Yagami-san said. "This is nasty business. Any idea how strong that monster you attacked was?"

"I'd say around level 20,000."

"This dungeon is at least A-rank, then... It isn't realistic to fight our way to the surface with them."

Yagami-san and I turned our eyes in the direction of the civilians who were visiting the park moments ago. There must've been sixty of them, and most were bunched together, chattering in chaos and confusion.

"What just happened to us?!"

"Can't you tell? We got sucked into a dungeon!"

"Are monsters gonna attack us? Are we gonna die?!"

I didn't blame them. Even for veterans like us, this situation was jarring.

"We should probably find a way to calm them down first," Yagami-san said.

"I think you're right."

"It won't be easy, but the saving grace is that we're here to help. There's a small chance we can get everyone out alive."

"...*Our* presence is a saving grace?" I murmured to myself. Something felt strange.

"What's wrong?"

"It's nothing."

I said that, but I couldn't help but tip my head and mull over the *unnatural* feeling in my gut. Two things had happened back on the surface: first, I felt that bloodlust; second, the dungeon outbreak swallowed us like prey. Was our presence here a "saving grace" or was it because of someone's ill intent? I had my doubts, but no way to confirm them, so I kept quiet for now. The best move to calm these people down was to tell them that members of the famous Yoizuki Guild were here to help.

But before we could, a rumble echoed through the room. The civilians immediately panicked.

"What's that?!"

"A horde of monsters?!"

The sound resembled the one that hounded us in Onizuka when the monster swarm occurred. In fact, the room we were in opened up into two tunnels, and as I focused, I sensed monsters marching through both of them.

"First, we need to figure out beating this horde," Yagami-san said.

"Right. Your party should handle that tunnel. I've got this one."

"You're not trying to stop that side alone, are you?! There must be at least...two hundred, no, *three hundred monsters*!"

I nodded. What was the point in pretending? Given my level and experience, I didn't think I could coordinate attacks with his party well. Easier for me to handle them on my own.

I summoned Speed Sword into my right hand to dual-wield it alongside Greed. These were easier to wield than against weaker opponents than Nameless. Yagami-san watched me for a moment, then relented.

"All right, you cover that side. Call for help the second you need it."

"I will."

We separated and took our positions chipping away at the monster stampede. Luckily, the narrow tunnels funneled the monsters into waves, so I only faced about ten at any given time, but there were *hundreds*. Worse, their levels ranged from 15,000 to 25,000. I fought defensively and didn't hold back on a single attack.

At first, I held to my basic agile fighting style, but there were more monsters than I imagined. Once the tide started pushing me back, I had to rely on Time Zero.

My MP was around 85,000. Time Zero cost 100 MP a pop, which meant it would run out pretty quick. As overpowered as it was in a one-on-one battle, I realized in that fight how poorly suited it was for large-scale extermination. Even so, I couldn't yield. I held steady against the battering tide for five tense minutes.

"You're *it*!" I shouted.

I cut down the final monster, which cleared my tunnel. I turned to the opposite tunnel, where Yagami-san was prepping a spell.

"Prominence!" he yelled.

A stream of fire barreled into the tunnel and swallowed the horde, reducing their numbers to zero. That tunnel was narrow too, so they managed to beat them all without much struggle.

The civilians chattered nervously.

"I-it's over..."

"I couldn't see it all, but it's safe to say they defeated the monsters for us, right?"

"Are we saved?"

They were unable to do anything but watch us fight, and they couldn't comprehend the deadliness of the situation we were in. We'd held off this first wave, but that wasn't the same as being *saved*. Without knowledge of dungeons, they didn't know better.

They were trapped in a terrible, life-threatening situation.

Now that we'd defeated the monsters, we adventurers gathered at the center of the room.

"It's great that we endured this attack and all, but answer me honestly," Yagami-san said. "How many more times can you manage a fight of this caliber?"

Everyone stayed quiet, including me. Even with my attempts to keep MP waste to a minimum, I'd lost over 60,000 points. Everyone else probably felt the same strain.

Yagami-san grimaced at our reactions. "Should've known. Then, it's impossible to escort them to the surface."

"We won't know unless we try!" one of the tanks said.

"We *do* know. I used Enemy Detection during the battle, and my guess is we're on the final floor. If my hunch is right and this is an A-rank dungeon, we can assume there are sixty floors total. We're not making it that far."

"So what do we do? Twiddle our thumbs until another monster wave attacks?"

"Of course not. We have two options: hold off the monsters until help arrives or challenge the boss monster together and trigger the return spell."

Everyone's eyes shot open wide at his second suggestion.

"Are you nuts?!"

"I don't *love* the second option, but if we're gonna do it, we better do it soon. We need to go in with as much HP and MP as possible," Yagami-san replied.

In my opinion, the second option was the *only* option. People without stats wouldn't gain rewards from beating the dungeon, but the return spell would teleport them out. If we used that function to our advantage, we might get everyone out of here alive.

The plan came with risks. If the boss defeated us, everyone would be wiped out. The more cautious option was to endure the monsters and wait for help, but if we waited, *who* could possibly help us? Only an S-rank adventurer was powerful enough to challenge a brand-new, irregular dungeon on the fly.

"There *is* someone who could rescue us..." I murmured.

The radiant image of Claire came to mind, but I immediately brushed it away. After I defeated Onizuka with Yagami-san's party, she explored it thoroughly and won the takedown rewards. She was subject to the Span. Unlike the guild party, which was swallowed directly by the outbreak, Claire couldn't bypass the Span. We only really had the one out.

Rumbles began to echo through the tunnels again.

"It looks like there's no more time to think," I said.

Yagami-san clucked his tongue and set his expression. "If we had a few more minutes, we could've formed a plan, but all bets are off. We decide *now*."

"Does that mean...?"

"Yes, I think we should go to the boss room. Except—"

He stopped speaking, so I met his eyes steadily.

"Amane, whichever choice we make, I'll probably end up depending on you. Will you give me your opinion?"

My mind was made up. "Let's face the boss."

"Okay. We'll get moving," he said. "Everyone, escort the civilians. There's no time to waste. Threaten them if you have to so long as they follow us. If there's any heat afterward, the responsibility is on my shoulders!"

"Yes, sir!" we responded.

We explained the situation to the civilians while the sound of monsters thrummed in the distance. Together, we'd enter the boss room with the goal of reaching the Return Zone. Most of them opposed going *toward* danger, but once we informed them every adventurer was about to leave the area, they reluctantly followed.

Enemy Detection revealed to us that the boss room was close. We would reach it with a few minutes of walking.

"Yagami-san's party, take the lead and break a path through the monsters! I'll take the rear!" I called.

"I'm counting on you!" Yagami-san replied.

They marched ahead, the civilians close behind. Hana, Rei, and Yui were behind them, and I stood at the very back.

In a group of nearly eighty people, we carved a path to the dungeon boss.

The trip was about five minutes long, as predicted. We eliminated any monsters that attacked and reached the boss room without casualties. Once there, Yagami-san ushered everyone inside.

"Hurry, oniichan!" Hana shouted. Everyone but me was huddled inside.

"Coming!"

I cut down one final monster and made a break for the boss room as the giant door groaned to life. I squeaked in just a second before it slammed shut behind me. I took a breath, but my relief was short-lived as I took in the room itself.

My eyes widened. "What in the world...?"

A starry sky stretched above us, complete with a glittering full moon. A garden full of flowers—heck, a *pond* too—stretched all around us. I couldn't believe what I was seeing, but what astonished me most stood behind the garden.

"Seriously...a *palace*?" I wondered aloud.

It was enormous. The flowers and pond I could get past. Dungeons often had unique fields for their monsters, sure, but why was a bona fide *palace* inside a dungeon? This was totally unprecedented, far as I knew. After all, *monsters* didn't live in palaces.

There was one more thing. Ten balls of fire formed a ring that floated high above the palace, illuminating it.

"What's going on?" someone shouted.

"I don't know! I've never heard of anything like this!"

Everyone was baffled, and most watched in silent horror. I couldn't form words either. I knew I should move, but I was stuck trembling as the fire danced and spun toward us. It started to coalesce into *something* as it descended. Instinct told me to avoid touching it at all costs.

"Don't tell me *that's* the boss."

As I spoke, the fire formed the outline of a body. More murmurs, hushed by terror, rose from the group.

"No way..."

"Is this even possible...?"

In simple terms, it was a creature of pure flame. Its expansive, carmine body was at least ten meters tall—taller than a three-story house—and made entirely of crackling, scorching fire. It radiated searing heat upon its surroundings.

My gut screamed that we needed to run and run *now*. Heck, I had the highest level in the room and that was what *I* would do. The creature's aura alone was beginning to knock the civilians unconscious.

It hit me then...our failure. We should've stayed out there and taken our chances with the horde. There was no going back now. If we didn't beat this thing, we'd all die.

I used Appraisal. Searing, honest misery flooded my vision.

IFRIT

LEVEL: 100,000

DUNGEON BOSS: [Unknown] Dungeon

"An ifrit...!"

The name of an S-rank monster—the very first one I'd ever faced in battle.

AMANE RIN

LEVEL: 39,852   **SP:** 34,910

TITLES: Dungeon Traveler (10/10), Nameless Swordsman, Endbringer (ERROR), Wiser Wise Man

HP: 312,830/312,830   **MP:** 59,340/85,690

ATTACK: 73,810   **DEFENSE:** 62,480   **SPEED:** 77,770

INTELLIGENCE: 61,550   **RESISTANCE:** 61,840   **LUCK:** 61,070

SKILLS: Dungeon Teleportation LV 29, Enhanced Strength LV MAX, Herculean Strength LV MAX, Superhuman Strength LV MAX, Endurance LV MAX, Adamantine LV MAX, High-speed Movement LV MAX, Gale Wind LV MAX, Enhanced Spirit LV MAX, Tenacity LV MAX, Revitalize LV 1, Purification Magic LV 1, Mana Boost LV MAX, Mana Recovery LV 2, Enemy Detection LV 4,

Evasion LV 4, Status Condition Resistance LV 4, Appraisal,
Item Box LV 8, Conceal LV 1, Battle Barrier LV 5, Plunderer LV 1

SWORD OF THE NAMELESS KNIGHT

A sword used by the Nameless Knight.

RECOMMENDED EQUIP LEVEL: 10,000 (MAX)

ATTACK +100%

When an enemy (human or monster) is of a higher level than the
wielder, all parameters except HP and MP increase by 100% each.

MAGIC-STEALING SHORT SWORD, GREED

A reward given to those who defeat the Remote Magic Tower.

RECOMMENDED EQUIP LEVEL: 33,000

ATTACK +72%

When magic strikes this blade, the wielder may pay MP equivalent
to the cost to cast the magic and absorb it. The absorbed
magic may be activated at no cost.

STORAGE CAPACITY: Maximum seven types.

CHAPTER 7

SILVER AND BLUE

NAMELESS KNIGHT. Orc general. Lightning beast. Yanagi. High ogre.

I'd defeated so many intimidating enemies thus far, including ones that were double my level. My unique arsenal—Nameless, Greed, and Dungeon Teleportation—had helped me gain the experience to overcome them. Maybe those fights were miracles, like falling on thin ice without cracking it. This boss's level was almost triple mine, a matchup so uneven that I felt like my miracles had run out, leaving me with only despair.

How could I fight *and* protect a crowd of vulnerable people? Non-adventurers couldn't stay conscious around overwhelming mana for long, so it wasn't long before they had all collapsed to the ground.

These were the worst possible conditions to fight under.

I was powerless.

But...I couldn't quit without *trying*. I just couldn't.

I knew this wasn't a typical enemy as soon as I saw it. That spurred me to make a big decision. I withdrew a collection of magic items from my Item Box.

FORTIFYING MEDICINE
Strengthens the body and decreases damage by 30% for 60
    seconds.
COOLDOWN: 10 minutes.

"Yagami-san, distribute these to the adventurers," I said.

"Is this the Fortifying Medicine? *And* enough for everyone?" he asked, stunned. "But you only beat that dungeon once, and it only rewarded one of these. How did you get this...?"

His words tapered off. He must've suspected what secret I was hiding. At least that made the conversation easier.

"Please, create a barrier," I said. "That way the civilians won't get caught up in the battle."

"...'Course we're gonna do that," he said. "Matsumoto, Misaka, you heard him. Form a defensive line!"

"Roger!" Matsumoto said.

"Yes, sir," Misaka replied with a nod.

The two mages took position, but we knew a measly magic barrier wouldn't stop the ifrit's attacks. The barrier *would* prevent the ifrit's dense mana from smothering the civilians. Without intervention, the mana was enough to kill them.

I turned the other way. "Hana, Rei, and Yui, you three shouldn't fight. Group up with the others."

"Okay," Hana said without question.

"I really, really don't get what's happening, but I trust you, Rin-senpai," Yui said.

They hurried inside the barrier, but Rei lingered, a pained expression painted across her face. A moment later, she followed. I felt terrible, having heard her desire to support me just a short time ago, but she couldn't participate in this fight.

All three of them had superior talents. Rei had Magic Sword—the ability to create swords with different abilities. Hana had Stock—the ability to copy anyone's skill. Yui had her healing knack—the high aptitude for any sort of Recovery Magic and Enhancement Magic. Regrettably, these skills weren't enough to take on the ifrit. Even Yagami-san's party was shaking with fear.

And so was I, but I *had* to beat it.

The ifrit moved. In the center of its burning face, it opened two sparking, golden eyes. They seemed to roll until they focused on their target: me.

"Sensing the highest-level adventurer in the group, huh?" I said. "Gee, I'm honored. Battle Barrier!"

BATTLE BARRIER LV 5
By draining MP, this skill creates a mana barrier around the target. (The strength and duration of the effect changes according to skill level.)
COOLDOWN TIME: 60 seconds.

Once Battle Barrier was set, I sprinted a half-loop around the ifrit. I was a bit far from the others, but this way, the fight wouldn't sweep them up.

The ifrit released an air-shaking howl as it watched me dart past it. It swung its arm with unnatural, elemental speed disproportionate to its huge size. *Uh-oh.* The flames of its arms unwound then twisted into a hammer-shaped fist. I sped up and narrowly dodged. The fist slammed into the ground no more than a meter away.

In an instant, my vision turned crimson.

"What?!"

Its fist triggered an explosion so powerful, the word didn't feel sufficient. The strike created a shockwave and left behind a crumbling crater that crackled with fire in its wake. The fervent heat of the fire incinerated the garden's delicate flowers and evaporated the lake. The stifling heat made me break out in a sweat at a distance *and* with Battle Barrier in play. This monster was *nasty*. One hit from this thing would roast me into charcoal or maybe scorch me straight to the bone.

What could I do? How could I defeat such a mighty enemy?

Think. The second I stopped thinking was the second I'd lose. Our makeshift party wasn't powerful enough to win without outsmarting the ifrit. I was starting to feel stuck when an idea popped into my head. In the aftermath of its hammer attack and the follow-up explosion, the ifrit's arm seemed...bare. I thought its whole body was made of fire, but it had a fleshy, susceptible body beneath the whirl of flames.

If it had a solid body, physical attacks *would* work.

That still isn't enough. I need to figure out how to break through that wall of fire.

Stealing the fire cloak with Greed, like I had against the salamander, wasn't an option. The MP loss would be horrific, and
there was no certainty I even had enough to pull it off. I wasn't
even sure I could do it at *full* MP.

Could I attack the arm during the time it came down and the
fire exploded? Attacking the arm wouldn't kill it...but that was all
I could do right now.

The ifrit roared and lifted its arm again.

"Now!" I shouted.

I made my move as the arm slammed down. Nameless sliced
into the tough hide. It was hard to push through—but not impossible. It would definitely deal damage, but nothing fatal.

"Amane! Above you!" Yagami-san shouted.

"Time Zero!"

The other arm slammed down milliseconds after I teleported
away.

A combo attack, huh? It seemed the ifrit didn't like me running circles around it. Evasion was my specialty, so I wasn't going
to take a hit lying down.

"I've gotta win this," I said to myself. With my courage bol-
stered, I darted toward the ifrit again.

Our stalemate dragged on. The ifrit launched its two-arm
combo and unleashed bursts of fire. I evaded them with Time
Zero and attacked when I had an opportunity. Yagami-san's party
intermittently used magic to distract it. I couldn't let the ifrit
actually attack them, though, so I constantly struggled to pull its
attention back to myself.

As we fluctuated between offense and defense, I monitored the ifrit's movements to figure out where the magic stone inside its body resided. Every single monster had a magic stone. Destroying the magic stone might kill it faster than dealing damage.

I didn't love using this method because destroying a magic stone meant destroying a valuable item—not to mention destroying the monster's body and the lucrative parts that came with it—but this situation was too dire to consider the opportunity cost. Getting out *alive* would be the real reward. Accounting for my lack of power and the ifrit's enormity, this was the last method available to me. But as I searched for the right moment to attack its weak point, something else interrupted.

"*Grrroooooooohhhhh!!*"

"What the heck?!" I exclaimed.

The ifrit reared its head back in a sky-splitting bellow that shook the room and pushed down on us with a physical pressure. The bellowing was intimidating enough, but the real threat followed. Part of the ifrit's fire pulled away from its body and knitted into an orb above its head, hot and bright and blazing like a sun, big enough to eclipse the false moon hanging in the sky. The incandescent glow saturated the boss room in light and heat. It didn't exactly feel like a pleasant campfire.

The sun ruptured into dozens of pieces that plunged from the sky with the force of a god's iron hammer.

You've gotta be kidding me!

Each sunshard contained an *obscene* concentration of mana. They mercilessly rained down on us like a meteor shower.

I see.

This beast hadn't even touched the big guns before. It knew we were too weak to pose a real challenge, but we'd put up more of a fight than it expected, so it decided to wipe us out in one move. It must've really hated *me* because about 80 percent of the fireballs were descending my way. I desperately dodged each one, but while I evaded direct hits, the overpowering heat melted my surroundings into a sea of fire wherever they landed.

Once I had a second to breathe, I turned my attention in the opposite direction. "Is everyone okay?!"

The tanks absorbed the initial impacts, but they'd taken severe damage—everyone was splayed on the ground. One huge, final fireball descended toward them.

"Like *hell* you will!" I screamed.

I activated Time Zero and moved to them. At the same time, I summoned Greed into my left hand and braced for impact.

"Eat it!" I shouted. The action stole 30,000 MP, but I was just relieved it stole the fireball too. "Is everyone okay?!"

"Y-yeah. You seriously saved us," Yagami-san grunted in a strained voice. He knelt on the ground, battered and bloodied. Seeing his injuries spurred me to a decision.

"Go inside the barrier," I told him.

I recalled my actions during my fight with the lightning beast and decided that, in this do-or-die situation, I should take the Fortifying Medicine. Once I swallowed it, I approached the ifrit from the front and quietly said: "Time Zero."

A moment later, my vision went black—proof that I'd infiltrated the ifrit's body.

I still had no idea where the magic stone was located, but I didn't have time to be precise. If I couldn't destroy the magic stone, I could inflict damage from the inside.

I started choking.

Why? Oh, no!

Smoke and heat filled my throat through the cracks rapidly snaking across Battle Barrier. It was awful—the ifrit's insides burned like the fires of Hell itself!

The shock of it spurred me to activate Time Zero. I reappeared in midair, but I was nearly too late. A moment longer and I would've roasted in there.

I fell to the ground and landed on one knee, drawing the ifrit's searing stare. Hana and the others still huddled to the monster's right, but it only seemed interested in menacing me. Its face twisted like it was telling me it wouldn't allow a parasite like me inside its body.

"Same to you, buddy!" I spat.

I struck myself in the chest, smashing my damaged Battle Barrier to pieces. The sixty-second cooldown had already passed since I first activated it, so I summoned it again. This way, I cloaked myself in a flawless defense.

The plan I thought was my secret weapon failed. I had only one option left. I'd run at full speed, faster than the ifrit could imagine, while Battle Barrier protected me. Then I would strike the ifrit before its fire could torch me!

I took a deep breath, then released it with a yell as I took off. No gimmicks this time—I ran at full tilt. The ifrit snarled angrily and launched a fireball at me. I was already moving too swiftly to turn, but it didn't matter.

I initiated a single attack that used every fiber of my being—*accelerate, teleport, penetrate*. I called it Invisible Slash. I outran the fireball and chain-teleported into the air.

"Take this!" I yelled.

I swung Nameless viciously, cutting through the fire and scoring a deep gash in the ifrit's chest. I felt resistance—I was *sure* I did.

"Huh?"

Something struck my left side. My mind blanked. Battle Barrier shattered in one blow and the heat flooded over me like lava. The impact threw my small body so hard, my back slammed into something. One of the starry walls? I could feel blood pooling beneath me after I crumpled to the ground.

The HP bar at the corner of my eye dropped below 10 percent.

I lifted my head and saw the ifrit as if through a fog. Its murky shape shook out its right arm.

Oh...it punched me and...sent me flying...

I coughed, adding another splatter of blood to the dungeon floor, but I wasn't down for the count yet. As my eyes refocused, I saw the ifrit clutched the gash in its chest with its left hand.

Yes. I definitely dealt damage. One more hit—if I could land just one more hit, I could really beat this monster!

"Rin!"

"Oniichan!"

"Rin-senpai!"

Rei, Hana, and Yui shouted from behind me as I rose, ignoring my wounds. I couldn't stop. If I did, everyone else would have to fight the ifrit.

"Ngh!"

Each step sent shockwaves of pain through my body. I wanted to collapse on the spot. Worst, during the time it took me to rise, the ifrit had begun its next attack. A giant sun swelled above its head again, somehow larger than the last one.

"Not like this!" I hissed.

That much fire would undoubtedly envelop us. Everyone would die.

Everyone but me.

I could use Time Zero and leave the boss room *now* if I wanted to. I could survive. Heck, I already knew a strategy I could use to beat the ifrit once I was back. If I used Time Zero and Battle Barrier while I evaded and showered it in attacks, I could deal enough damage, no problem. It'd be a tough fight, but this monster was out of surprise attacks. There was a good chance I could win.

That would only happen if I let the others die—a Pyrrhic victory. No matter how hard I tried, I couldn't win *and* protect the others. But what was the point of a win like that? The whole reason I was *here* was to get Hana and everyone else out alive. They were too important to me.

Man, I'm still so weak.

Why did I want all this strength? If I can't protect them here, there was no point in obtaining it!

I glared at the ifrit's golden eyes. "Listen up, beast. Aim everything you've got *right here*."

Hana and the others were too close to me, so I dashed away from them. Battle Barrier wasn't active. I had nothing to protect myself with, no hidden strength left to tap into, but still, I raised my blade! Even if those flames burned me to cinders, I would save the others!

"Wait!"

A clear voice rang out, but I had no idea who it belonged to. My everything was focused on was charging the ifrit.

Faster. I have to go faster.

I pushed past my limit. My HP was below 30 percent, so Revitalize kicked in. I sped onward. And then—

There was the sound of breaking glass, then that voice again.

"Cursed!"

It happened so quickly.

The deafening sound of shattering reached my ears, then the sound bounced through the space, compounding on itself. I— *everyone*—looked up at the sky, where cracks splintered through the heavens. A gash burst open and split the ifrit's artificial sun in two. As the two halves separated, the full moon beneath revealed itself.

"No, that's not it..." I whispered. Not the full moon. What shone there was a woman with a flash of luminous silver hair.

Kisaragi Claire.

The sun, its energy rent apart and destabilized, exploded.

Dozens of fiery fragments scattered everywhere. Pieces of it raced toward us, but Claire whispered something again.

"Cursed."

Her voice sounded so cold, it could've frozen me to my bone marrow.

As she said the word, she swung her ice sword. It emitted a cold wave that devoured the hellish fires. Snowflakes bloomed and drifted through the air as she landed smoothly beside me.

Questions piled in my mind: How was she here during a Span? How did she destroy the boss room ceiling? Could she stop the ifrit? I had no idea where to begin.

"Compared to the exterior, this was much easier to penetrate. Very fragile," Claire said casually.

I stared, completely dumbstruck.

"I apologize for the delay," she said. "Entrust me with the rest."

Claire spun on her heel, bowed low, and aimed the point of her sword at the ifrit.

"Absolute Ruler," she commanded.

She summoned an ice magic circle around herself, large enough to surround me, Hana, and everyone else too. Massive amounts of mana spilled from it.

"No way!" I gasped. Our near-fatal wounds had healed in the blink of an eye. That wasn't all. The healing effect fully restored my HP *and* MP. Was that possible?!

"Claire, what is..." I began, finally finding a question to start with, but I couldn't finish it. It didn't seem to matter as much as her elegant beauty, the snowflakes framing her like stars as she brandished her sword of ice. The sight of her from behind unexpectedly overlapped in my mind's eye with the memory of the adventurer who saved me all those years ago.

"You might not know what you're doing," she told the ifrit, "but I can't allow you to harm them anymore." She fixed her severe blue gaze upon the creature. "I will exterminate you."

That's when I witnessed what the strongest of us could *really* do.

I had to wonder what the ifrit felt, seeing Claire appear out of nowhere. It snarled with a ferocity it hadn't aimed toward the rest of us, as if it recognized a true threat posed to its life. Five new suns rose above the ifrit's head. Each one was connected with a thin stream of flame that drew a pentagram. It radiated the most scorching heat we'd felt so far.

"Out of my way," Claire said in a low voice.

Her blade flashed. The suns froze over and the ice fractured into snowy powder, as if there had never been fire at all. This moment proved the exact disparity between the two of them, and the ifrit must have realized how outmatched it was. It abandoned its five-sided star, set its sights on *us*, and released a forceful stream of flamethrower breath.

"Do you think I will permit that?" Claire sounded dismissive.

The ice magic circle glittered with light and formed a barrier of thick, interconnected glaciers to protect us. The flamethrower attack slammed into the glaciers but failed to penetrate them.

The ifrit screeched in frustration and stepped backward. It must've expected to rattle Claire and use that moment to damage her, but it knew now it had no hope of victory. Claire inhaled slowly, then said in her iciest voice, "Now, let us finish this."

Her preamble done, Claire flipped her ice sword, Cursed, into a fighting position. She struck in a decisive upward arc. A monumental sweep of ice left her blade and froze everything in front of it, air *and* fire. The ifrit was hit dead-on: even its tough skin couldn't withstand her power. Its flesh was artfully bifurcated by her ice. The wound revealed the magic stone in the ifrit's brow, and the cracks that laced through it. A moment later, it fractured into bits.

I gaped.

Was what I glimpsed even *real*? I stared at Claire's back in a stupor. Her domination of the ifrit was absolute.

"Gained XP: Level increased by 923!" the system said in my mind.

The system recognized that I contributed damage to the defeat, but I didn't care about the level boost. Claire's moonlit silhouette held my complete attention as she looked at the ifrit's toppled form.

"It's over," she said, turning around.

Our gazes met like two blades clashing together. For a second, her eyes widened and she halted, but then her expression softened and she resumed walking, until she came to a stop in front of me. She extended a white-gloved hand. The strong extending a helping hand to the weak. My heart thumped as I saw it.

"I, uh..." I stuttered, but I didn't know what to say, so I settled for taking her hand.

The warmth I expected was drowned out by a menacing shadow that loomed over us. We whirled toward the source simultaneously—the palace, the most abnormal thing in this space.

A man stood there.

Since when was he there? He'd appeared silently, as if he was there from the start. His eyes and long hair were the same color as freshly spilled blood and he wore an ink-black coat. The aura he carried was even stranger than his appearance. He didn't seem stronger than the ifrit, yet he emanated a malignant air that the ifrit hadn't.

I couldn't say why he was so threatening. Whatever the reason, I *knew* this man was more dangerous than the rest of us.

"Amane-san, is he one of the people swallowed by the dungeon outbreak?" Claire asked.

"Definitely not. He just appeared."

The man's sharp gaze snapped to us, and instantly, I realized that I'd never *seen* him before, but I'd felt his *presence*. How could I forget it? It was right at the onset of the outbreak.

The source of the bloodlust I felt was *him*.

I drew Nameless and slid into a fighting stance. Claire did the same with Cursed.

The man remained unconcerned as he smiled and started toward us.

"What a surprise," he said. "I've been watching the riffraff fall to the ifrit from inside the palace, and just when I thought this world was a waste despite its purported development, someone delightfully *strong* shows up. You'll be a bit of a hassle to take care of, but I suppose it's better than crushing ants all the time."

"Who are you?" Claire asked.

"*Hmph.* Since you're a lovely little thing, I'll tell you."

The man halted, grinned, and dropped a piece of information like a guided missile into our understanding of the world.

"I am the vampire Cain Fon Vertia. To make it easy for you simple-minded folk to understand, I am a being from another world."

Cain's words made everyone's eyes widen in surprise—even Claire's.

"A being from another world...?" she echoed. "Are you speaking sincerely?"

"Naturally, I am." He gestured to himself. "You truly haven't noticed? The mana that cloaks us is completely different."

"Let us say I believe you," Claire offered, "why would you be *here*? Too many things about this situation are unbelievable, this abnormal space included."

"My presence should speak for itself. I merely overwrote ownership of this dungeon when it spawned and designated myself its ruler."

Something was off about his phrasing. Claire's doubtful expression indicated she was with me. Her posture stiffened. "Then, you didn't create this dungeon?"

"Clearly not. That's the work of God. Even a being such as I cannot manifest a dungeon."

Overwrite. Ownership. God. I couldn't let go of any of those words, though they were spoken so casually. Was this "God" of Cain's the system's voice? Was he saying that the dungeon system had a singular will behind it? What was this *another world* stuff anyway? Assuming it was real, what role did dungeons play in that other place? We needed a *hint* of answers to keep us from drowning in questions.

One thing *was* clear: We were getting closer to the truth behind dungeons.

I would have to quench my thirst for knowledge later, because something else took immediate priority. I didn't know what Cain meant when he claimed he "overwrote" part of this dungeon, nor what "ownership" was in this context. What I *did* know was that Cain was stronger than I was, yet he sat and watched while the ifrit brought us to the brink of death.

That said everything about what kind of man he was.

"Fine. I have many more questions, but I will settle for the answer to one," Claire said. "Why have you come to this world?"

Was that *Claire's* voice leading the interrogation? She spoke so neatly and coldly to the ifrit. This tone, echoing with rage and hatred, was remarkably different. Somehow, her voice didn't move Cain at all. The corners of his mouth curled upward like a Cheshire cat, as if he'd suppressed his emotions the entire time and was about to crack.

The dam burst, spilling out in a wave of malicious laughter.

"Fantastic question! I have but one goal. Send my troops into this world via dungeons, eliminate its human inhabitants, and take over the world, my pretty lovely little one."

Whump. I felt Cain's mana balloon to the same level as the ifrit's in an instant—proof that he was ready for war.

"Dammit!" I cursed. I swiftly raised Nameless in opposition, but Cain moved faster. He summoned at least ten blood-red magic circles around himself.

Claire circumvented them.

"Pardon me," she said. She was the picture of cool-headed ruthlessness, swinging her sword faster than I could count. After each magic circle lay ruined and unable to activate in her wake, her next target was Cain's throat. "Haaa!"

Cain clucked his tongue in frustration. "Blood Wall!"

Ten walls of blood appeared in the space between them, a barrier of red. Claire slashed through them one by one but grew slower each time. When she reached the last, she was forced to a standstill. Her eyes narrowed in dissatisfaction as she dodged back from some unseen force.

"You can defend against me?" Claire said.

"Fine words from the girl cutting through my prized Blood Walls!" he countered.

"Don't you have other abilities at your disposal?"

"Who knows? *Do I?*"

The two of them glared at each other. I didn't feel anger or panic as I stood nearby; I felt *reassured.* How could I feel anything else? Yes, Cain was strong. Easily as strong as the ifrit. But

watching him and Claire go head-to-head proved how incredible Claire was. I couldn't hope to take Cain out on my own, but Claire could definitely defeat him. It was a huge weight off my shoulders to know I wouldn't have to fight this powerful enemy. I could support Claire from the sidelines and protect Hana and the others.

So I thought. In reality, my trial was just beginning.

They looked like they were prizefighters sizing each other up, but they were actually building mana for their next attacks. Claire's aura dwarfed Cain's. He snickered when he noticed the disparity.

"That's some *frightening* power you've got there. What you deployed against the ifrit was the proverbial tip of the iceberg, hmm?" he mocked. "I'm sure I have no chance against you in a duel...but unfortunately for you, time is up."

"Time is up?" she asked. "For what, exact—"

"No!" I gasped.

Claire and I widened our eyes, unable to believe the sight before us. A soft glow wreathed her body. We both recognized it as the activation signal warning she'd soon be teleported to the Return Zone.

That much was typical. She defeated the ifrit, the dungeon boss. The unbelievable part was what *wasn't* happening.

"Why is it only working on Claire?!" I shouted, losing my cool.

That light should've enveloped our whole group. Me *and* everyone else. But it didn't. Claire was about to get sent to the Return Zone, leaving us with this *villain*!

This isn't happening, this isn't happening, this isn't happening!

My head nearly exploded from the torrent of denials flooding it.

"Call it my backup plan," Cain said. "When I took ownership of the dungeon, I rewrote the rules. The one who defeats the dungeon boss goes back to the Return Zone, meaning you, *girlie,* leave alone."

Was that even possible...?

Wait... Yeah, when Claire defeated the ifrit, the system only told me that I'd gained XP—nothing else. No takedown rewards at all! I couldn't even conceive of how much power Cain held as the "owner," but that surprise was quickly replaced with numbness. Something far more urgent demanded attention: Cain. He was strong, stronger than the ifrit, and he planned to execute us. If we lost Claire, who could beat him?

"Claire!" I cried, reaching for her, praying that she wouldn't disappear. Claire gripped Cursed tightly. Her expression was conflicted until her eyes widened and focused on...me.

Why? Why me?

I was nothing compared to her. What did she see in me when we locked eyes?

Claire flipped Cursed over and stabbed it deep into the ground.

"Absolute Ruler!"

A magic circle expanded from the sword and swathed everyone except me, Claire, and Cain in a barrier of ice. She took one last look at me and whispered, "They're in your hands."

The glow surrounding Claire flared into blinding light. When it receded, she was gone. Our only hope of defeating Cain had vanished into thin air.

I held my empty hand aloft.

As I stood, rattled, Cain turned to me and spoke with saccharine cordiality.

"Is this an ice barrier for protecting the powerless? Sadly, then, that leaves you and me," he sighed. "Foolish girl, entrusting this bout to a weakling. You'd best not waste energy on hoping she'll find help, by the way. The Gate closed the moment she arrived. I'll crush you worms long before you can try to wriggle away from me."

Cain's sanguine glare burned with such venom that it threatened to stop my heart on its own. A chorus of worried voices rose up behind me, but the ice barrier flattened the sound to a hush.

That ice separated me from them, which meant the only person who could protect any of us was...

"Me," I breathed out.

Their lives were in my hands again, and I was against an enemy stronger than the ifrit I'd failed to defeat. I had no hope of winning, not even a scrap. Hopelessly, I stepped forward to do battle with malevolence incarnate—with Cain—anyway.

CHAPTER 8

THE TYRANT AND THE KING

CLAIRE, OUR ONLY HOPE to defeat Cain, had vanished in a flash of light.

Cursed was stabbed solidly into the ground, its ice barrier enfolding everyone but me and Cain. The blade pulsed like a living organism; the barrier throbbed in rhythmic response. The barrier was still forming—it was drawing upon Cursed's power, I suspected. If the blade left the ground, I was sure it would destroy the magic circle and take the barrier with it.

Claire's last gift. She left it behind so I could focus on defeating the enemy. It *had* to stay put.

They're in your hands, she told me.

Without her here, I was the only one with a fraction of a chance of winning, but *how*? He was stronger than the ifrit, an enemy that already bested me. I didn't see a single path to victory.

Think, Rin. Think!

I had to keep thinking until I pieced together how to beat him. To buy myself time, I started questioning Cain.

"Why won't the teleportation spell work on us?" I asked.

"I *just* told you. I'm the owner of this dungeon, so I modified its configuration."

"You said 'God' creates dungeons. Are you saying you're allowed to seize ownership from a god?"

"Please, young man! I'd never lay claim to *all* of it. I simply limited who may leave after the dungeon boss is defeated. Besides, once I eliminate everyone in this room, it will empty out. The result will be the same."

I stayed silent.

"I can't change a predetermined system twice. If you want to get to the surface, you'll need to kill the owner—*me*—and obliterate the dungeon itself."

So, if Cain died, the dungeon would be destroyed. That made an owner something akin to the final boss of a dungeon collapse.

I held onto a flickering hope that everyone would return to the surface alive, but the odds of managing it were near zero. As much time as I bought to let my ideas run in the background, I never came close to a winning strategy.

That wasn't even the worst part.

"Are you kidding?!" I exclaimed.

The crater in the ground, the scorched flower field, the evaporated pond, and the broken ceiling... Like an unwinding clock, they restored themselves until the boss room was as pristine as it was when we set foot inside. I'd never seen this happen before. The flames that hovered over the palace restored themselves too, which meant once they combined, they'd transform back into the ifrit.

"You have *got* to be kidding me!" This was getting ridiculous.

Cain laughed, enjoying my frustration.

"I must inform you, *worm*, you weren't the only one passing time," he taunted.

"How'd the ifrit revive itself?!" I demanded.

"More tiresome questions. The little miss wasn't the only challenger here, remember? The boss will respawn to battle any interlopers. You should know that."

My mind rushed to deny it but arguing couldn't help me now. My miniscule chances of winning dropped below zero if Cain *and* the ifrit attacked at the same time.

I grit my teeth. The ifrit suddenly roared and brought its fiery arm down, but more surprises lay in store—the ifrit wasn't aiming for me. It was aiming for *Cain*.

"Blood Wall," he said.

A thick wall of ruddy coagulated blood materialized to swallow the hit. The impact sent an explosive sound and an accompanying wave of blood through the near vicinity, but it protected Cain perfectly.

"Surprised?" Cain asked. "A boss will even turn on the dungeon's owner once it respawns. If I were inside the palace, I wouldn't have to deal with this...but no matter. I won't let it get in the way of our fight. Now, *bow down*."

Hundreds of threads of fresh blood shot from Cain's hand and spun toward the ifrit. They knitted around its body and dragged it down to the ground. The ifrit, now immobilized, screeched in anguish.

"There. That should prevent any interruptions to our battle," Cain said. "I have no qualms with allowing you to die at its hands but...well, I'd hate to waste such a perfect opportunity to taste the experience of someone from another world."

I clicked my tongue in annoyance. The side show was over.

Cain, clad in crimson mana, threw a smirk my way. "The time has arrived for me to crush you under my heel, *child*."

With those haughty words, our battle—one I had no chance of winning—began.

He was right. He was very easily crushing me under his heel.

Ten magic circles floated around him, each one firing crimson magic in my direction. The forms varied: blades, spears, bullets, and arrows, all of them emerging from the circles with enough power to kill me.

"Ngh... *Time Zero!*"

With Time Zero activated, I could avoid each attack by the skin of my teeth. Any ground my feet touched was obliterated by his magic a millisecond later. I raced through a storm of booming sounds and debris, just to get away from his bloody weapons.

Cain roared with laughter. "What's the matter? Can't handle my bloodsucking magic? No shame in that, no shame at all! I'm in a different league from *mere insects*!"

I couldn't object. I wasn't moving too fast to speak—I straight up didn't have the mental bandwidth to spare on retorts.

His magic struck closer with every attack, and distressingly, he'd started to anticipate where I'd teleport. I couldn't afford to be at more of a disadvantage than I already was. I had to attack while I had the strength!

"My turn!" I shouted, and took the shot, Nameless gripped tight in my hands.

I used teleportation to circumvent his magic circles and charge in for the kill. I channeled all my momentum into Nameless and swung.

"Attacking at last, are we?" Cain said. "I'm afraid you're not quite up to par, *worm*!"

Clang!

My pulse rocketed at the sound, while my body slammed to a total halt. Cain's Blood Wall had interrupted my attack at the last possible second. My blade was half submerged into the bloody mass and wouldn't budge no matter how hard I pushed.

I'd dodged those attacks for a single strike, and this was where it got me. *All right. Time to try something else!*

"Greed!" I shouted, summoning the short sword into my left hand. I pulled Nameless out and readied my grip for a stab attack with Greed.

It didn't matter how strong this Blood Wall was. So long as it was made of magic, I could steal it.

"I hate to be the bearer of bad news, but your fight with the ifrit exposed *that* trick!" Cain said.

"*What?!*"

The Blood Wall vanished faster than Greed could pierce it.

I struck air. The lack of resistance sent my body tipping forward, leaving me wide open to his kick. Teleportation wouldn't bail me out; I twisted Nameless to intercept instead. The sharp impact of his boot slamming into Nameless ricocheted through my body, tearing a grunt from me. I'd successfully softened the blow but was pushed onto the backfoot as a result.

"More where that came from," he promised.

Having forced me into the most vulnerable stance of my adventuring career, Cain pursued me like a shark who smelled blood. He summoned a fresh set of magic circles, massive ones that stretched across the room. They covered the space so thoroughly that I had nowhere left to teleport.

I clenched my teeth. Should I use Greed? No, Greed had a storage capacity of seven spells, and those circles spit out more than it could handle. Besides, considering my MP limitations, I couldn't absorb them all. Dodging was the only choice I had. I evaluated the scope and power of each incoming spell.

"Argh!"

I ducked the fatal spells, but the weaker ones slammed into Battle Barrier. Phew. Miraculously, I managed to get out of that round blissfully unscathed.

"Well, this is a surprise!" Cain said. He sounded genuine. "You survived, but what impresses me is that you minimized the damage. A pushover like you must have struggled against a fair few overpowered opponents to manage that. How long will those survival skills keep you afloat, I wonder?"

Cain's ego wasn't affected in the least by his miscalculation. Instead, he summoned his next round of magic circles. *Tsk.* I'd have to escape another barrage.

How did he use magic so fluidly anyway? His bloodsucking magic was flexible—he could attack *and* defend with it at will. The mana cost must've been extreme. Was he pulling mana from a supply source? If so, where?

One possibility hit me.

"Don't tell me..."

I turned to the ifrit. The hundreds of threads Cain cast to bind it kept it pinned flat on the ground. Cain could be drawing upon its blood and the mana stored within. The puzzle pieces fit together too well.

Cain claimed he didn't want the ifrit to interrupt our battle, but that didn't add up. He knew the ifrit would spawn during the fight, but he had plenty of methods to protect himself, so why not let it rampage? I would be at a much steeper disadvantage in that scenario, obviously. Then, he was suppressing the ifrit for a *reason*. My guess that he was using it as a mana source looked increasingly likely.

"Right..." I murmured. "Hence the *bloodsucking*."

Talk about a tricky power. With its secret out in the open, it would be easier to deal with. I turned my sights to the ifrit. I should defeat it first.

When Claire bisected the last one, she revealed where its magic stone hid. I had a chance!

I took off at a run.

"Oh? Caught that, did you?" Cain called. "Well, I'd reconsider my battle plan if I were you. If you defeat that beast, you'll be whisked straight to the Return Zone as well."

I hit the brakes and skidded to a stop. He was right. If I trusted what he said about the boss room's rule, whoever defeated the monster would return to the surface alone. In Claire's case, she only had about a minute before the teleportation spell kicked in. That left *one minute* to defeat Cain, and if I failed, Hana and everyone else would be stuck with him. Nope, that method was off the table. The risk was too high.

I can't live with myself if I screw this up!

"Good boy," Cain said. "Stay still where you are, so I can *stomp* you into the ground."

The onslaught started anew. I bobbed and weaved away from the magic circle attacks as I pondered my next move, my MP chipping away bit by bit with every swerve. I didn't have time for this. This was do or die.

Think. Think! THINK!

There had to be something in my bag of tricks that could defeat him. Any idea would do. There was some way to overcome him.

Come on. Remember.

I recalled the misplaced feeling that struck me when I first saw Cain. Overwhelming fear tempered with the strange realization that his power was *lower* than the ifrit's. His aura only felt stronger than the ifrit's after he released the crimson mana. There was something else—the impact when he tried to kick me and hit Nameless instead. Sure, I'd blocked it, but I expected more damage. That didn't match up with an S-rank attack. This left me with a theory.

Are Cain's stats fundamentally weaker than S-rank?

Nameless's effects kicked in around him, so he definitely *was* stronger than me, but that didn't guarantee he was S-rank! His bloodsucking magic was a powerful unique skill, not wizardry. If the scale of his mana source was what boosted his abilities, there was a good chance I *could* defeat him.

If I could get one solid hit in—just one—I could end this!

"There's only one way I can pull this off," I muttered.

Riding high on the hope of escape, I put the rest of the plan together in my head. I had one shot at fooling Cain. I needed to pour everything into this attack, in a way he'd never see coming!

Gripping Nameless in both hands, I stared Cain down. He clearly noticed some shift in me. He flashed a bold grin in return.

"Whatever idea just entered your head won't work. Your blade can't reach me."

"I won't know that unless I try."

"Oh? Then go right ahead. I'll obliterate every last shred of your hope, human!" Another sickly red flood of magic circles raised around him.

Here goes nothing,

I ran straight for Cain. I wove around his spells as I sped forward, accelerating with every passing second.

"Ha!" he snorted. "That's the same plan you had last time! It won't reach me!"

A dense and presumably impenetrable Blood Wall manifested between us. Time to use Time Zero to get him from behind? No, he was definitely anticipating that...but that was the key to my plan. I ducked low and pulled Nameless back as if it were a javelin—tightening my back, shoulder, elbow. The movement forced all my momentum into my arm. The second that Nameless's point touched the Blood Wall, I said, "Switch."

Nameless instantly swapped places with Greed in my hand. *This* was my final turnaround attack: Switch Penetrate. He'd take it for granted that his Blood Wall would block my attack. He was too cocky to prepare for a sword to break through! It was over!

"Ahhhhhh!!!" I screamed as I threw myself into the attack. The Blood Wall bent inward as Greed devoured it. I pushed forward—until Cain captured me by the wrist.

"Wh-what?"

I paled. *This* was unexpected. How did he guess? Did he actually prepare himself?

"I knew you would do that," he chuckled.

"Relea—"

"Nice try, fool!"

Frantically, I attempted to release the ifrit's fire that I'd stored inside Greed, but Cain kicked me square in the stomach and sent me flying so fast my vision spun.

"Gah!"

As I rolled, I could see the fire spell burst from Greed...in the wrong direction.

"Now die," Cain said.

Before I could utter a word, a wave of fresh blood crashed into me.

I don't know how many spells battered into me then.

The first few broke my Battle Barrier, then they smashed through the Blood Wall I desperately released from Greed. The rest of them struck me directly.

Under the onslaught, my senses failed me. I was hit from behind, from the front, from *everywhere*, until I was flat on the ground with something cold against my back. Too late, I remembered the ice barrier that protected Hana and the others. I only realized where I was because the sword Claire had left beside me—Cursed—was there.

The HP gauge in the corner of my vision—which maxed out at over 300,000—showed only 1,000 HP left.

"Your plan wasn't bad, but unfortunately for you, I already predicted how you would fight," Cain said. "It's impossible for you to beat me."

My mind was hazy with pain and barely capable of understanding his words. I'd fought so many powerful enemies—the orc general, the lightning beast, just to name a few—with greater physical abilities. Even people like Yanagi, who could strategize on par with me. Cain was the first one who possessed *both* qualities. In front of him...I was just some weakling trying to cheat a victory. He wouldn't even let me step foot in the ring.

The ifrit hadn't made me feel half this desperate.

I understood now what *utter defeat* felt like. No matter where I went, there would always be someone much, much stronger. I was insignificant. The strength I'd worked so hard to gain was as fragile as glass—

"*Rin.*"

A voice broke through my melancholy, stopping the final piece of my heart from breaking. Had it come through the ice barrier? It sounded muffled, but I was positive someone said my name.

My heart awoke again. It leapt.

As scared as I was, I couldn't turn back. I had no choice but to battle Cain. What must they be feeling, watching me from the sidelines? I owed them an apology for letting them down.

I turned around to see Rei's face—and many others—through the glass. "Huh?"

Their eyes weren't dull with hopelessness. Their faces were pained, as if they were frustrated by their powerlessness—but they still believed in me.

"Why...?" I asked. I was useless, even during the battle with the ifrit. I couldn't believe they still had faith in me. "How can you...?" *How can you believe in me?*

I just *didn't get it*. I was weak. I didn't have the power to protect them. Why did they have so much faith in me?

And I remember...Claire had faith in me too.

Taking in everyone's eyes, they wore the same expectant look that Claire had.

Her words echoed back.

They're in your hands.

She'd saved me from the ifrit. She had even protected everyone with her ice barrier before she was pulled out. She was the strongest of all of us. Why did she think I was capable of taking the torch she held out to me? I doubted I could ever follow in her footsteps. I'd never have the power to protect everything.

I was weak.

I must've gotten arrogant somewhere along the way, after Dungeon Teleportation *truly* awakened and helped me level up faster than anyone. Call it coincidence that I managed to save some loved ones here and there. I'd gotten wrapped up in my own growth and convinced myself I was special, but at the end of the day—I was a worm, just like Cain said. I couldn't do anything by myself.

I understand that so well, it hurts.

Despite that, and every negative thought I was so certain of, some things just couldn't go unaddressed. I dragged myself, insignificant as I was, off the floor. Blood winnowed down my body in thin streams as I stood, but the feelings of the people behind me and their sense of longing fueled me. They told me not to give up.

Everyone who Claire had protected resented their weakness. It was all they could do to watch. But only I had the ability to fight back! I wouldn't give in so easily!

I hated my own weakness, but I couldn't let it eat me alive. It was simple: I wanted to protect the people I cared about. That was all that mattered. They believed in me despite my insignificance. I wanted to make them proud!

So I—

I—

"I want *power*."

Even if it burnt me to ashes, I prayed for the power to beat Cain—for strength like *Claire's*! From the depths of the pit of despair, one light shone above me. The image of a girl with silver hair.

I reached for *her*.

Cain tensed as he watched Amane Rin crawl.

Rin had taken near-fatal wounds, but he'd been in similarly dire straits when he challenged the ifrit. Animals were all the more ferocious when wounded, or so the saying went. Cain didn't let his guard down for a moment. He readied another charged barrage of spells—only for Rin's next action to catch him completely off guard.

"What are you...?"

Rin wrenched the silver-haired girl's abandoned sword free from the ground. As he did, the protective ice barrier behind him shattered into nothing. Rin didn't pause to enjoy the spectacle; he sprinted away at once, his silver sword in his right hand, the ice sword in his left.

"You'd abandon your allies to launch a suicide attack...?" Cain pondered.

For the first time since they'd met, he couldn't sense what Rin was thinking. Cain could no longer rely on instinct. The rest of the adventurers were still too pathetic to waste time on. Rin's inexplicable actions were more intriguing than a crowd Cain could kill at any moment, so he focused on Rin alone.

That is, until Amane Rin *vanished*.

There went his teleportation skill again. Cain fell into a defensive stance, ready for wherever Rin might reappear, but the move was pointless. Rin bypassed Cain altogether and headed for the ifrit, which was the last thing Cain had expected. By the time he realized Rin's target, it was too late to act. Rin cleaved the ifrit's forehead with the ice sword, destroying the magic stone and extinguishing the fire that cloaked the ifrit. In the aftermath, he stood motionless on top of the corpse.

Despite losing his mana source, Cain didn't flinch. He fixed Rin with a glare.

"I was wondering what your plan was...and then you went for the ifrit," Cain sighed. "You know, cutting off my mana source isn't going to stop me. Or did you decide to return to the surface alone, even at the cost of the ice barrier protecting your friends?"

"I'm not going anywhere," Rin said. "Removing this sword is my vow to protect them instead. Besides, I have the power I need to defeat you."

"...You *what*?"

Unease prickled at Cain like pins on the back of his neck. Rin's posture shifted into something entirely new, as though his spirit itself was transformed. Without meaning to, Cain stepped back.

Am I retreating? No, of course not. The change is some trick of the light...some flight of fancy. Our difference in strength is clear. Attitude can't overcome that!

Cain wrapped himself in a cloak of red mana then propelled it upward, focusing it into a concentrated point in the air above. Rin would soon see how misguided his ambitious little ploy was.

"You can't talk *this* away. All of you are as good as dead," Cain said. "Perish at my feet! *Bloody Lightning!*"

Fresh blood with the branching shape of lightning crackled through the air. Rin's teleportation skill might allow him to evade such attacks, but it was impossible for him to protect the others at the same time. He didn't have that kind of power.

This is it!

A wide grin split Cain's face as his spell crashed down.

Rin knew the blood lightning magic was a death sentence, but he clung to the memory of a certain silver-haired girl's heroic stance, nevertheless. He admired her, yearned to become like her, to be someone with enough power to protect everything and everyone. He hoped such a burning desire to grasp strength would lead him there someday, but for now, he was a novice. He *couldn't* protect everything. He didn't have the power.

Yet, he tried all the same.

I might not be up to protecting everything, *but I want to protect everyone close to me.*

He would do what it took to conquer despair.

Dungeon Teleportation, LV 30.

Next were the words that changed the world.

"Piece Ruler."

The hundreds of spells descending on him vanished without a sound. In a flash, they reappeared to surround *Cain*.

"Is this some sick joke?!" Cain cried. His eyes practically bulged out of his skull.

In a matter of seconds, Cain lost his status as the hunter and became the prey. He summoned a Blood Wall to defend himself, but there were too many spells for it to counter the extent of them. Many of them lanced into his skin. As blood fell around him, dust welled up and blocked him from Rin's view.

When it dispersed, Cain emerged bathed in blood from his own magic. His eyes glinted with fury as he glowered at Rin.

"You little schemer! You *didn't* kill the ifrit to run away!" he accused. "You killed it for the *experience*! You've leveled up some skill with the power to control magic!"

Rin pointed the ice sword toward him without a word, as if he felt no obligation to answer. In that room, in that moment, another ruler was born. This new ruler declared his will to Cain with a quiet yet decisive decree.

"It's time, Vampire King. With everything I have, I will *destroy* you."

A fathomless whirlpool spun in Rin's blue eyes, waiting to drag Cain to the bottom of the abyss.

DUNGEON TELEPORTATION LV 30

SUB-SKILL: Piece Ruler

By paying MP equal to the mana of the target object, the user
may teleport anything in sight. This ability cannot be used on
people, monsters, or equipped items.

DURATION: 10 seconds

COOLDOWN TIME: 10 hours

CHAPTER 9

A SMALL GLORY

OUR BACK-AND-FORTH left me bruised and beaten, but I was glad Cain and I could finally fight toe-to-toe. My new ability to use *everything* around me as a weapon meant the battle got a whole lot harsher for him.

Our magic tug-of-war sent shock waves through the area. The effort tore guttural sounds out of my chest. Incredibly, Cursed's energy flowed into me each time I used Piece Ruler to teleport Cain's spells, as if replenishing the mana I'd paid. The mana that went into maintaining the ice barrier was now mine to use as I pleased. Was it working this way because its owner wasn't here? Or was something else at play?

The pulse of mana pouring into my body brought searing pain with it, but I didn't flinch—I couldn't afford to. I knew that retreating to breathe would make my advantage crumble like a sandcastle at high tide. Instead of falling back, I used the pain as a foothold and urged myself onward.

Cain was losing his temper. "Impossible! There's no way my

strongest spells can fall apart like this! You won't get away with this for a *moment* longer!"

He could tell instinctively not to approach me. No matter how many times I seized his magic, he didn't give up. He cast spell after spell: fifty, one hundred, two hundred, *five hundred*. It was a volley of magic, though he didn't fire them at me. His targets were Hana and the others.

"I won't let you," I said. I'd sworn to protect them. *If I can't steal all of those spells at once, then...*

"I'll cancel it out!"

Cain spluttered in shock, but what could he do? I seized half the spells as they were cast and swerved them directly into the remaining half. Bursts of wind and sound tore through the space where they made contact. I darted across the battered battlefield and drew close to Cain—close enough for my blade to reach. I *swung*.

"Curse you!!!" Cain seethed. He retreated in an armor of rushing blood.

He'd picked up that I couldn't teleport equipped items. Dang, that was fast. The armor blocking my blade felt dense and much stronger than the Blood Wall.

So what, so what, so what? I'll get through it, and anything else in my way!

I roared with the force of my strikes on his armor. My two blades flashed—one silver and one blue. The combo attack sang faster than the speed of sound. The silver and blue light blended into one beautiful color. The giant arc they formed slammed into Cain and pushed him back.

Revitalize's effects offered me a hefty benefit, so I had something of an edge in close combat. I expected as much. Cain tried to retaliate with magic, but I seized control and slapped his spells aside.

"This can't be!" Cain roared. "No power like this can feasibly exist—argh!"

Cain's blood armor disintegrated at last. He was defenseless.

One more strike. One more strike and I've got him!

Piece Ruler's time limit was almost up. Everything hung on my final attack. I swung Cursed, throwing my weight into the strike.

"You think you've won?!" he shrieked. "Think again!"

What I saw next turned me numb with shock. Blood sprayed in the air, but not from *my* attack. Cain's right arm whirled upward. A magic circle glimmered in the stump where his arm had been, and soon enough, a spear composed of blood disgorged from inside of it. The spear didn't rip his arm off to stand in for it. To my astonishment, it fired right at me.

I couldn't believe it. This guy sacrificed his own right arm to attack my blind spot!

The result was devastating. The spell consumed the entirety of my vision before I had time to process what it was. I didn't teleport it in time, not remotely. The blood spear knocked Cursed out of my grip and lanced Battle Barrier, shattering it in one hit. I was vulnerable to a lethal strike.

Another hit would end me.

I stepped forward, dauntless. *No time to regroup. Now or never! Do or die!!!*

I raised Nameless and swept it through the air, but Cain was not ready to die either. He transmuted the blood that gushed from his severed arm into the shape of a blade.

We clashed blades at a blazing pace, bellowing in unison.

Our blades slid against each other with a sharp, shrieking sound. The flow of time seemed to slow. I realized that Cain's attack was a fraction faster than mine. His surprise attack must've slowed me down just enough for this to happen. Teleportation wouldn't save me. Cain's blade was about to cut my life short.

So what?!

Kill me, then! I'd keep my grip tight through sheer force of will and ensure this would end in *mutual* destruction—

A soft yet powerful voice rang out.

"Magic Sword."

A lash of wind whipped up out of nowhere and bent the trajectory of Cain's blood sword.

"What?!" Cain gasped.

Out of the corner of my eye, I saw her—the brave girl who sent that burst of wind.

Kurosaki Rei.

I understood, then. How could I forget? I wasn't alone. The others lamented their powerlessness, but they rose up beside me regardless. We were never alone in our battle against despair.

The sword Rei swung so courageously hardly held a candle to Cain's, nor did it successfully block his attack, but she bought me a millisecond of time that was worth an eternity. It was exactly what I needed.

Our gazes met. Her eyes bore into mine with determination. "Go on, Rin," she said.

I've got this.

Time and I both raced forward. I shouted with the release of momentum as I slipped past his weapon and slashed with my silver blade. I had just enough time to slice deep into his body. Blood gushed out of him, a lethal amount, I was sure. His eyes widened at the sight, as if he couldn't grasp why his blood stopped obeying him. His ward evaporated as the strength to maintain it drained out of his veins.

"No. I...lost?" he breathed. "To a pathetic weakling like *you*...?"

"Maybe we *were* weak, but that's precisely why we can get stronger. Our ability to grow means we're not powerless at all."

"You...ah...I see. A powerful person such as I can never understand your position," he rasped. "If that ignorance is...the root of my failure...so be it. I must accept..."

Cain faltered and slumped to both knees. His eyes were vague and unfocused as he said his final words. "At least tell me your name."

I hesitated before saying, "My name's Amane Rin."

"A *warning* to you, Rin," he replied. "Don't...don't think my defeat will bring you peace. Your *true* hell...is only beginning."

His body desiccated and crumbled away, as if the dungeon itself absorbed him.

The system rang out, proof that we defeated Cain and triumphed over hopeless odds.

"Rin!"

The girls cried my name. Relief that I'd managed to protect all of them hit me hard. So hard...and then...

Meanwhile, during Rin and Cain's battle...
Above ground, Claire cursed her own uselessness.
How is this protecting anything?
She'd vowed to protect everything and everyone, so how was she *here?* Her hands clenched into fists so hard, her fingernails drew blood from her palms. The cuts healed over in seconds.

Curious onlookers had gathered to gawk at the dungeon that spawned out of nowhere. Claire stood like a captain at the helm of the crowd. They were all perplexed at the one inexplicable feature—or lack thereof. Like any dungeon, this one should've had a Gate, but it didn't. It simply wasn't there. No matter how strong the adventurer, no one could get inside.

Claire couldn't.

Unable to follow the desire inside her to save everyone, she stood, burning with frustration. What had happened minutes before, when the light of the teleportation spell enveloped her, played on a loop in her head.

In that fraction of a moment, she'd tried to defeat Cain before the spell fully activated. She'd failed. Her original plan was to reenter and reach him again. The grim flaw to that plan was... everyone else would be dead by the time she reached the boss room a second time.

From where she stood in the present, stuck on the surface, one part of the memory rose in her mind.

She'd defeated the ifrit and turned around, meeting Rin's eyes. He hadn't looked resentful or angry. She could tell he regretted his powerlessness, his helplessness, but he'd still had light in his eyes.

Seeing that perseverance in him, she'd chosen a different option. Instead of the plan where she bore everything herself, she'd entrusted the rest of the fight to him and left Cursed behind, counting on him to protect the others.

After that, the teleportation spell had taken her aboveground, away from the thick of battle.

Now, the dungeon had no Gate. If she'd chosen her first plan, the outcome would've been unthinkable. Though leaving Cursed with Rin was the better choice, the decision didn't sit right with her. She'd sworn to protect everything on her own, but that better choice put her here on the sidelines.

I failed to protect anything again...

A vulnerable, pained expression overtook her face, but her melancholy was interrupted when someone in the crowd shouted.

"Hey, somebody came back!"

She gasped and looked up, where she saw Rin swaying, battered and beaten. He crumpled as if he'd just lost consciousness.

"Amane-san!"

She dashed for him and caught him before he hit the ground.

Why was he alone? Her heart leapt with fear, but quickly settled in her chest. As he leaned against her, his face broke into a satisfied smile. She didn't know what had happened inside, but she understood the meaning of that smile. He'd successfully protected everyone.

"Thank you," she murmured.

She cast healing magic on his wounded body. She was glad to see his wounds heal, though having him slumped against her like this was an ungainly burden. She couldn't lay him on the hard ground either.

Well, she supposed she didn't mind letting him rest with his head on her lap. Slowly, she lowered him into position and stroked his head, hoping he felt her gratitude.

"You did well, Amane-san," she said gently.

She wasn't sure if she imagined his small smile.

Several minutes later, the dungeon collapsed, and those still trapped inside at last returned to the surface. It marked the end of a long, *long* day.

THE WORLD'S FASTEST
LEVEL△UP

EPILOGUE

"**W**HERE AM I...?" I croaked.

I opened my eyes to a clean white ceiling and fluorescent lights.

I understood then I was in the hospital. But why was I there? My memories were still catching up to me when someone spoke.

"Good morning, Amane-san," Claire said.

"...Huh?"

I turned my head to find her sitting at my bedside, peeling apple slices. Most people would make bunny ears out of the peels, but she had carved Wolfun's ears instead. Wow, her work was really detailed... *Wait, no time for that!*

"Where is everyone?" I asked as I sat up in a hurry. "Are they okay—*ack!*"

Pain racked my body as the details hit me. I sank back into the bed.

Claire started and moved her hands in a settling gesture. "Calm down, Amane-san. You were severely injured and shouldn't move. They're fine, thanks to you."

Then I *did* manage to save them. I breathed a sigh of relief.

"How long was I out?" I asked.

"Three days, more or less."

"Three *days*?!" That was about two and a half days longer than I expected. "Why are you here peeling apples if you didn't know when I would wake up?"

"Yui-san and the others eat them when they come by to visit, so I thought it wouldn't hurt."

Oh man, if they were well enough to visit me in the hospital, that meant they were perfectly safe. I was glad to hear it.

That left one more important topic. "Can you tell me what happened after I passed out?"

"Certainly. Once the dungeon collapsed, everyone was returned to the surface. They were transported to the hospital for precautionary exams. Even the civilians who fainted from the strong mana exposure turned out fine."

"That's good. What about Cain?"

"Oh, the man who claimed to be from another world? I gave a report to the Dungeon Association. Given the circumstances, it won't be made public yet. They will wait for the right moment. In the meantime, only the highest-ranked adventurers were informed."

"Figured they'd do something like that."

Dungeons harbored so many unknowns. The whole *world* had tried to understand them, but we were left grasping at theories and little else. If people found out another world existed with sentient life that was intentionally targeting us, society would fall into chaos.

"Amane-san, can I ask *you* a question?"

"Sure."

"I heard from Rei-san and the other girls that you used Cursed. Is that true?"

"It is. In fact, your sword is the reason we got out safe. If it weren't for the mana your sword gave me, my MP would've run out."

Claire's eyes widened. *"What?"*

Had I said something wrong? "Was it not okay to use the sword?" I asked.

"N-no! If it assisted you, then that's...all that matters. Please, do not concern yourself further."

"Well, okay..."

Honestly, I wanted to ask *more* after her reaction, but I left the subject alone. She obviously didn't want to talk about it. We'd covered what we needed to cover. Quiet draped over us. I drifted in and out of awareness, time flowing past us like a clear stream...until Claire waded into the silence and pulled me back to wakefulness.

"Amane-san."

"Hmm?"

I blinked up at her face, then lost all words. Her smile hinted at sadness, but it was still as captivating and beautiful as a sunrise over the ocean.

"Thank you so much," she said. "If not for you, no one would've survived."

"Why would you need to thank me for that?"

"...I suppose I don't, but I thought I should."

Her somber expression reminded me of our conversation at the café ten days ago. She looked like she did back then, when she said it was her duty to protect everything. Was she thanking me because I protected them when she couldn't? If she felt like she was useless back then, that didn't make any sense. Something in her voice nagged me. I wanted to know more.

"Claire—"

"I think I'll be in the way if I stay here any longer. I should head home," she interrupted, standing and turning away.

I pictured her stance when she defeated the ifrit. She seemed unbreakable—a strong contrast to the Claire whose shoulders now slumped with the weight of the world. How could I *not* be curious about what weakness she perceived in herself? Did she believe her duty was to protect everything *alone*?

Her words were as clear as day in my memory.

"Your goal is well on its way to being realized."

"You think so?"

"No, I know it. And once you do realize it, I hope you'll be..."

She trailed off after that, but was she about to say what I thought?

I had to tell her something. No—I *wanted* to tell Claire something.

Just as she reached for the door, I rose from the bed. "Wait, Claire."

"Amane-san? You shouldn't move!"

"I'm okay. I can handle it."

Back at the café, I couldn't bring myself to push, but I could do it now. I didn't know what burden she bore, but I could at least tell her my own feelings.

"I'm the one who should thank you, Claire," I said. "We were only saved because you came to our aid. Your strength is in a league *way* beyond mine."

"My strength..."

She looked troubled. By now, she must've received a lot of praise for her strength. It made sense that my words didn't mean much. What I *really* wanted to say came next.

"That's why I want to catch up to you," I said.

"P-pardon?"

"I want to become strong enough to protect everything too. If I need strength like yours to do that, then I *will* catch up...actually, wait."

That wasn't quite right. It wasn't *enough*. I'd sworn to become the strongest adventurer in the world.

"Once I meet my goal, I'll find you there. So, wait for me, Claire."

Surprise lit up her bright blue eyes.

Ugh, I sounded egotistical, didn't I? I didn't even say it for her, more for myself. Despite that, or perhaps because of it, it seemed to strike a chord with her. For a second, a wet shine glimmered in her eyes, but then she smiled.

"I'm sorry, but your declaration will never become a reality," she insisted. "I'm going to get stronger too, you know."

"Guess I'll have to level up even faster than you, won't I?"

"Well, then...let's make it an official challenge, Amane-san."

"You're on!"

Bright light filtered into the space between us as we made our vow.

We hardly knew each other, but that didn't matter. We understood better than anyone else that the promise we made was real. As for the many questions yet to be answered, well...we trusted time to teach us.

After all, our story had only just begun.

LEVEL

44286

SP 29250

STATS

HP	348,400
MP	94,460
Attack	81,980
Defense	69,460
Speed	86,310
Intelligence	68,470
Resistance	68,720
Luck	67,920

ACHIEVEMENTS

Dungeon Traveler (10/10)
Nameless Swordsman
Endbringer (ERROR)
Wiser Wise Man

SKILLS

Dungeon Teleportation LV 30 (TIME ZERO / PIECE RULER)
Enhanced Strength LV MAX
Herculean Strength LV MAX
Superhuman Strength LV MAX
Endurance LV MAX
Adamantine LV MAX
High-speed Movement LV MAX
Gale Wind LV MAX
Enhanced Spirit LV MAX
Tenacity LV MAX
Revitalize LV 1
Purification Magic LV 1
Mana Boost LV MAX
Mana Recovery LV 2
Enemy Detection LV 4
Evasion LV 4
Status Condition Resistance LV 4
Appraisal
Item Box LV 8
Conceal LV 1
Battle Barrier LV 5
Plunderer LV 1

AFTERWORD

IT'S BEEN A WHILE, readers. Yamata here. Thank you for picking up another volume of my work!

I wrote Volume 3 with the intent of introducing new moving parts to the story, such as bringing in Claire—a major main character—in full force and presenting new mysteries behind the nature of dungeons themselves. That's why this volume has more action scenes than the previous ones. I especially packed a lot of heat into the duel with Cain, so it would be my greatest joy as an author if some of that heat managed to reach you, too.

That battle pushed Rin to make some huge strides. It was his first time facing a truly domineering opponent, which begs the question: Now that he's renewed his vow to become the world's strongest adventurer, what will Rin do next?

I hope you're excited to find out.

ACKNOWLEDGMENTS:

To my managing editor, S-sama. Thank you for sticking with me this long and pushing my work to even greater heights.

To my illustrator, fame-san. Thank you for producing such stunning art for Volume 1, Volume 2, and beyond! All of the characters look incredible, and I'm so satisfied with how the battle scene illustrations turned out!

Also, thank you to everyone else, including Suzumi Atsushi-sensei, who has taken charge of the manga adaptation; everyone involved with taking this novel from concept to the physical version out in the world; and the readers who have been with me from the beginning. You all have my deepest gratitude.

I hope to see everyone again soon.

—NAGATO YAMATA

FROM THE CREATORS

AUTHOR
NAGATO YAMATA

I live in Osaka and write web novels. Lately, I've been playing a lot of shogi.

I love tense battles where the main character of a light novel or manga series defeats a strong enemy. I incorporated many of those things into this book. I hope you enjoy it.

ILLUSTRATOR
fame

Looking at the cover art makes me want a snow cone.